Tristan Egolf was born in 1971. He ⟨...⟩ Paris, Philadelphia, New York City, ⟨...⟩ and for forty-eight mind-numbing G⟨...⟩ in Mississippi (where he's wanted o⟨... ...⟩. Along the way, he's worked as a dog-walker, a trash-truck cleaner, a projectionist, a janitor, and a boxing cornerman. His first novel, *Lord of the Barnyard*, was published to international acclaim; *Skirt and the Fiddle* is his second novel.

08/34.

From the reviews of Lord of the Barnyard:

'An hilarious masterpiece, one of the best debuts of the year from a young writer of formidable talent and imagination.'   *Uncut*

'A work of substance, significance and originality . . . it owes a discernible debt to Steinbeck and Faulkner, a more palpable one to John Kennedy Toole.'   *TLS*

'A wonderfully strange book . . . achingly funny and tragic.'
Literary Review

'A bold and original debut . . . his brilliantly warped, pedal-to-the-metal vision has the obsessive quirkiness of a Pynchon.'   *Salon*

'An exuberant bildungsroman . . . outrageous.'   *New Yorker*

'Ferociously imaginative . . . *Lord of the Barnyard* is an arctic blast of fresh air and a far cry from the formulaic writing so prevalent in much contemporary fiction.'   *San Francisco Chronicle*

'If Tristan Egolf were a circus artist, he would juggle chain saws.'
Cleveland Plain Dealer

'An outrageous, lyrical, jubilant epic . . . *Lord of the Barnyard* is a tornado of almost Biblical proportion.'   *Le Monde* (France)

'A singular new literary voice who is lord of his own universe . . . *Lord of the Barnyard* is a novel that, from the beginning, aims for the marrow.'   *El Pais* (Spain)

Skirt and the Fiddle

TRISTAN EGOLF

Atlantic Books
London

First published in 2002 in the United States of America by Grove Press, 841 Broadway, New York, NY 10003.

First published in Great Britain in 2004 by Atlantic Books, an imprint of Grove Atlantic Ltd.

1 3 5 7 9 8 6 4 2

A CIP catalogue record for this book is available from the British Library.
1 84354 220 X

Printed in Great Britain by Mackays of Chatham Ltd, Chatham, Kent.
Atlantic Books
An imprint of Grove Atlantic Ltd
Ormond House
26–27 Boswell Street
London WC1N 3JZ

Once I was an embryo,
Then I got the old heave ho . . .

—Shannon Selberg

BEFOREHAND

I was told nothing of the show beforehand. My agent never called. The union didn't warn me. The coordinator probably never knew I *existed* . . . From start to finish, I received no more than a fleeting message by way of Jane Doe: "*Yes, Mr. Evans — please report to the Balecroft Civic Center this evening at eight o'clock for a suit-and-tie affair . . .*"

A "suit-and-tie affair," she called it. The term induced panic. I spent all afternoon rounding up a tux, feeling more ill *equipped* than uninformed . . .

Seated on the southbound at twenty past seven. Chain-smoking Merits from station to station. Fiddle in lap. No other passengers. Power lines crossing the wall outside.

At some point, a tramp staggered into the car. He kicked a beer can, fell down flat. The doors hissed shut. The can trickled out. Beer pooled together in the floor-mat grooves. I watched it slide as the train pulled away, level off even in the blackened express lane, then track forward on deceleration, balling up filth, breaking new ground. I offered myself to its languorous crawl, void in the cease-fire, calm for a moment . . .

Slowly, the events of my week replayed. And a terrible week it had been, at that. From losing/relinquishing/quitting (I'm not sure which) my post at the Philtharmonic, to audits, the flu and receipt of a FINAL eviction notice by mail that morning, the only thing I *hadn't* managed to blow was my gig with the musical union.

Indeed, there are seasons and there are *seasons* . . .
This one made life in a squat seem rational.

—If ever I got out of Philth Town alive, bragging rights were sure to follow—across my chest in block capitals: I SURVIVED THE PORT OF EXTREMES. You could empty out pool halls in Lisbon on that. Or not. In truth—Christ, what a week— I SURVIVED BACHELORHOOD was more like it. And *that* was still pending . . .

A beat-up Timberland *stomped* into view. I jolted.
My rivulet died underfoot.
The Timberland shifted, edged into profile. Stricken, I locked to its gravel-torn shank and panned up from there, imploring Jesus—over an ankle chain, stonewashed pant cuffs, a windburned kneecap, a nickel-plated Harley buckle,

ring around the armpit, an undersize wife-beater, airbrushed, reading: SPEAK ENGLISH OR DIE—to a Bryl-maned, acne-pitted, craven-pallored bristle-snout with Ecto-mullet, dagger ring and service-station cap included. From there, back, for the overall picture: Postcard from Honky Town, 1984.

Sneering, he made his way to a seat and flopped down, akimbo—package on parade . . . He sucked down four long gulps of Schlitz, pitched the can and swiveled around—belching through foam-lined catfish lip growth, cussing to himself, glaring at the rail map, lighting a smoke with his butane knuckle bar, scowling at the tramp, plugging one nostril, craning his neck, snapping it, groaning, hawking phlegm, then cussing some more . . .

I gazed in wide wonder the whole way through.
What came next, Krishnas in Kevlar?

Set to write him off as a fluke when the doors slid open and three *more* appeared. Two males, one otherwise. Slamming a bottle of Old Crow. All a decade out of element—foul, mean, tough and nasty . . .

I shot to attention, *concerned* by now.

Okay, go easy—no cause for alarm. Hessians in Philth Town. Not *unheard* of . . .

Yet the next station brought four more of them. Soon to be joined by a pair at Elkins. Then a whole *crowd* farther on. Inexplicable: Keystone Dutch retrogression en masse. The car began to stink like a tractor pull in a heat wave . . . I kept wondering what kind of hole in time had spat forth on the sly. But more importantly—and this with a growing sense of dread—where these people were *going*? No one had gotten off the train yet, and there were only five more stops on the line. There was really nothing cooking in this part of town; after a certain point on the southbound, the area was no longer even residential—just storage lots and warehouse facilities. The only public venue was the Civic Center, and that's where *I* was going. So where did that leave *these* freaks? My agent wouldn't have let this happen. He wouldn't have *dared*, not with my record. Surely it *had* to be something else— some aberrant, regional faction in transit . . .

Even as the train neared the end of the line, I kept thinking: *Never—no way in hell* . . . But at the station, hope diminished. As we crowded the escalator, *fear* set in . . . With a host of inebriated longhairs around me and the roar of a mob from the exits above, I realized that, like it or not, our destinations were truly one and the same.

The platform arrived. A guard stood watching. I shimmied through the stiles with everyone else to join West Virginia's heated response to East St. Louis on a cast of thousands . . . Hessians *everywhere* . . . Jamming the divider strip. Mobbing the fence. In the middle of the road . . . Smashing bottles. Hanging from light poles. Climbing on car hoods, scrapping by the Port-O-Lets . . . A sprawling throng of Cro-Magnon havoc in every direction, for miles on end . . . Death rockers traipsing across the highway, *daring* coming traffic to get in the way . . . Vixens in leather, hair teased up to the overhanging heavens, *looking* for action . . . Carcino-mullets in roving squadrons, gobbing the

Red Man, cussing and yelling . . . Catfights raging out of control . . . Cops on horseback, lost in the swirl . . .

I hadn't known there were still enough Hessians to pack a stable, much less an arena. And this *was* their target—flocking to Balecroft as ravenous sharks to a capsized freighter.

Getting through was an absolute nightmare.

Picture one Cambodian/Negro fiddle stooge in a shrunken tux on a funky chicken through a mile of white lightning . . . wondering *what* he'd gotten into . . . hoping and praying there'd been a mistake, that he wasn't *really* supposed to be here—the guards would turn him away at the gate, throw him in a taxi or, better yet, escort him home in an armored wagon . . .

And, of course, I was due at the *farthest* gate—*clear* across in the opposite lot. Took *forever* to get there. And not *one* clue as to what lay in store along the way. It wasn't until Gate E loomed into view that a banner caught my eye.

THE RETURN OF VOLSTAGG

Volstagg?

It hit: a soured relic from adolescence—visions of tour shirts, tank tops, gold chains, feathered hair, cigarettes and beatings at the bus stop . . . And there, in the middle of it all, VOLSTAGG: corporate-Satanic Limburger metal, mono-browed Vikings in demon-seed black, traipsing along the edge of a castle with double-edged broadswords, *meaner than thou*. Avatars of a dead aesthetic, though apparently it, or *they*, were still alive. In fact, it would seem they hadn't even cut their hair . . .

VOLSTAGG.

This was the band's "comeback" tour.

VOLSTAGG RETURNS.

I couldn't remember any of their songs. As far as I knew, they had only *one* hit. Yet I guess that was all it took for a comeback. And, judging by the horde, they *had* been missed.

I could not fucking *believe* the union. Someone (my agent) would pay for this, dearly . . .

Four Sasquatches manning Gate E. I called one over, gave him my line. He asked for ID. I shook my head. Pausing, he thought about it, then gave in — clearly swayed by my suit and complexion. He opened the gate and shoved me in a corner. I stood near the wall as the ranks filed by.

Soon, somebody called me a nigger. Turning, I tried to single him out. But they all looked the same. Lost in Cumberland. How much *longer*, O Lord, how long?

I went back to watching the Sasquatches confiscate pipe after bundle after Carolina boot knife.

Then, more directly, it happened again: "GET GONE, COON!"—from a grub in fatigues.

And to think there was talk of sterilizing *pit bulls* . . .

I looked at my watch, thinking, *One more minute.*

"Pardon," came a voice. "Are you Charles Evans?"

I turned. He was small, balding, corporate.

"Yeah," I said. "Get me out of here."

"Sorry." He looked off. "Come with me."

Weaving, I followed his lead through the crowd. He drew a rope at the top of some stairs. We dropped the flight to a stage-room door. A techie opened up. I stepped inside. Three other union gimps were huddled in the corner. None familiar—to me or each other. We were given introductions with a careless nod, then handed our scores and told to prepare.

So, the long and short of it was this: not only were the four of us, as total strangers, expected to play before twenty thousand cases of arrested development off the cuff, we were actually there to play Volstagg's music—*un*accompanied, with-*out* the band, as the *opening act*—à la Johann Sebastian Bach: baroque renditions of shit-awful death epics . . .

I barely had time to rosin my bow. What little I glimpsed of the score was a travesty—incorrect signatures, misplaced codas, whole staff bars missing. Completely illeg-

ible. Random improvisation was one thing, but all-out blind
maneuvering?

Shit, sight-reading takes a *provisional* road map . . .
This was simply no damn good.

They drove us onstage at five till eight. We were
seated on a platform between two curtains. A techie appeared with our pickup cords. He signaled offstage. A
spotlight hit. Someone shouted to *move your asses!*

We never got a sound check — *or* a chance to tune.
The curtain went up with no further warning.

A startled surge of applause, more shocked than enthused, washed over the half-empty floor. It quickly died as
the stage lights rose . . . Four geeks in tuxedos. Nothing interesting. No VOLSTAGG . . . Everyone returned to the waiting game — catcalling, throwing trash and power-slamming
Miller Lite.

A blast of flatulence swept the stage. The cellist's hair
went amok, on end. The other gimps looked like Freedom
Rockers. A cone of blistering white enfolded us, down from
the skies: *You Have Been Chosen* . . . I shielded the glare for a
look around. But all I could see was a troll in the pit.

With bows drawn and a nod of collective surrender between us, off we went . . .

Our opening effort spluttered and ground to a ten-
second death. Which wasn't bad. The cellist reacted by sus-

taining our root, allowing us to regroup and proceed at the next measure. But back on track, it happened again. And then a third time. And once more by the end of the page . . . For lack of options, we stuck with the cellist, rolling along until trouble hit, then leveling off to a monotone lull. It sounded like dueling belugas wounded. Which isn't to say the audience cared. Right from the start, our lot was ignored. We didn't receive a single clap from a crowd of thousands the whole way through. We could've been playing *bluegrass* standards for all these people cared. No matter. The four of us remained in our own pathetic, miserable, inconsequential world—hacking and chopping through one catastrophe after another to *no one's benefit* . . .

Almost at once, a migraine hit. Soon, all four of us hit the boards . . . Nothing was in order. The monitors were shot. The stage lights, blinding—my scalp, half cooked. Someone had tampered with the soundboard, too, and the score just kept getting *worse* . . .

At one point the bassist went hopelessly astray and simply stopped playing altogether. He leafed through his book in a flustered panic only to find a whole *section* missing, torn out at the binding. He stormed offstage to demand another, then snarled and lashed at the curtain's edge. We continued without him, devoid of a low end . . .

Yet still, the crowd remained oblivious. Even as seats started filling to capacity, the only reaction we managed to elicit was a cry of impatience from a goon in the tiers. With whom we agreed. Enough was enough. At *least* forty minutes had passed by now. I couldn't *imagine* why the band was waiting. The stagehands were set. The mob had *been* ready. The four of us, useless—delay, without point . . .

A power chord blew from the rack overhead . . .

. . . Feeding, it rumbled across the arena: Godzilla rising from Tokyo Bay. The stage lights cut. Torches flared.

The crowd went apeshit, surging uncontrollably.
A carpet of vapors swept the floor.

Then another power chord. Behind us the curtain rose. Turning, I nearly flew off my chair . . . A giant skull with glowing emerald eyes slid forward on a rail track, hissing. A figure appeared between its fangs—Kull the Destroyer in lavender spandex . . . A cordless guitar rode his sagging gut. Several log chains hung from his belt. He jammed another power chord and *sneered* our way . . . The crowd went into overdrive. Someone threw a chair. The Destroyer kicked one platform boot overhead, spewing for all to assume: *Get that pussy-ass classical bullshit outta my face—VOLSTAGG is here!* And pretty soon the mob was booing us—throwing garbage, rushing the stage—egging the guards to *kill them faggots* . . . Another explosion signaled our cue. The four of us scuttled away in defeat—crushed, humiliated, *Killed By Death* . . .

Roaring, Kull the Destroyer swept our chairs and score stands into the pit, then spread-eagled himself to the horde with an outstretched sign of the beast.

❋

Goodbye.

❀　❀　❀

Six blocks north, I found a bodega. Went in. Grabbed a quart of Mickey's. Paid in change. Sat on the curb outside, drinking. Dupe in repose.

Minutes later, a squad car appeared. It slowed to a halt. The cop got out . . . I was searched, ordered to dump my bottle, grilled as a vagrant and written a ticket.

My least turbulent moment all day was still a societal crime, somehow.

When it was over, he drove away. I looked at the paper. OPEN CONTAINER. Casting it into the gutter, along with my fiddle, I walked.

To hell with it all.

THE DESMON

To look at it now, you wouldn't take Seminole Street for the heart of a once great district. It's hard to imagine this whole end of town, from Main to the river, as ever having prospered. Nowadays, the notion of the area's "golden age" would strike most locals as incomprehensible. Names like Pollup's Height or the Bartleson Market are gone with the splendors of yore—reduced to minor historical footnotes, along with seven eighths of the city . . . Whereas, in Athens or northern Jackson, at least a *glimmer* of the hoopla remains, on Glokland Row, the past is preserved through lack of proper demolition. With garbage and barrels and carts overturned in the streets, dopers at every corner, hundreds of empty storefronts locked and boarded and ongoing blocks in ruin, it's widely given the neighborhood surfaced DOA with the fall of Eden. Only the Desmon boardinghouse, Our Lady Kettlehole, stands to suggest otherwise.

When completed in 1920, this forty-room manor on Seminole Street overlooked the expanse of a thriving quar-

ter. Then, Dowler Ave. was a dining run, Twenty-sixth
Street, a fashion strip, the refinery lot, a public park—the
school yard on Holtz a botanical garden. Thousands of visi-
tors poured in daily. The streets were packed from dawn to
dusk. Dowler bustled into the evening. And after midnight,
speakeasies roared.

Times were good, it's all on file. There's even a book:
Pollup's Height! The Desmon's lobby is lined with photos. A
quick look around would bear out the myth—al*though* on
comparing a tintype portrait of the opening staff circa 1920
with a Polaroid of Jones, our deskman now, and his gaggle
of Argentinian maids, no one would make the connection.
The two establishments bear almost nothing in common.
The building's original brownstone facade, with its crenel-
lated balconies and broad center bay, would *never* seem fea-
sibly one and the same as our present-day billboard to public
neglect. The same holds true for the structure's interior and,
once again, the surrounding quarter. And as for the tenants,
well—the impeccably tailored swingers and germs of old
would hover not decades, but WORLDS away from the
Bottom-feeders in terminal currently.

❊   ❊   ❊

I moved in on September 19, ten days after the Volstagg
affair. Jones marked me down for room twenty-five, third
door in on the second floor. Each level was accessible by
staircase only; the lift had been broken for years, I was told.
Also, the roof was strictly off-limits. "Structural damage,"
Jones explained.

My room was a gray-walled eight-by-twelve with a frameless sleeper and torn yellow carpeting. An old pine desk sat rotting in the corner. A mirror hung next to the closet door. The window overlooked a weed-choked lot full of garbage and busted mattress frames. A pay phone and toilet were down the hall, a kitchen, shower and lounge below . . .

A long way down from my digs in Olde City, admittedly. Still, I couldn't complain. At $65 a week, it beat out pitching camp in an ATM booth.

Most of my neighbors were no better off. The Feeders were damned in utero, seemingly.

Across the hall lived Armless Rob, the house's token genetic anomaly, a literally armless computer programmer recently busted for corporate graft, whose oblong skull, offset by the crookedly stunted and winding length of his torso, made for the overall effect of a bloated gourd impaled on a broken fence post.

Right next door was Edwina (formerly Bruce) Selznick, a discharged air force attack-dog trainer who'd left his wife in rural Kentucky, moved to the city, had breasts implanted and taken up bouncing after hours at Peter the Conqueror's Hole of Iniquity . . .

Further on, we had Emmy Lou Mattressback, dominatrix extraordinaire, along with her "assistant," Yancey Fishnet, a starry-eyed hellcat from northern Maryland.

Then, in room twenty-nine, there was someone named Randy Beaumont, a rumored outlaw—a soldier of fortune in hiding, they said — whose end of the hall stank awfully of carp, whose hellhound, Finster, had mauled some ghoul, and whose girlfriend cleared six foot nine by report.

Those were just a few of the Feeders. Soon it would seem that we'd all been acquainted for years. At present, however, I knew only one of them: Tinsel Greetz, on the opposite wing — Tinsel, the neighborhood's leading dime-store anarchist goon and saboteur, Tinsel, who tailored himself as a modern-day Boxcar Willie, crust included, Tinsel, who blasted the everyday Joe as a slave to convention for holding a job, Tinsel, who couldn't have been more pleased to find me residing in Our Lady Kettlehole.

"*Took* you long enough!" he said that afternoon, eyeing my heap. "Now I don't have to be catching no train up to Corporate City for Breed retrieval. You didn't belong with those savages, Charlie. *And* your Realtor's a fucking Nazi."

"My Realtor?"

"Yeah." He frowned, nodding. "He's got the *pope* on his bumper, for Jesus'."

I suddenly felt less guilty about having set my kitchen on fire that winter.

"To hell with him," Tinsel continued. "One of these days we'll douse his Rolls in molasses."

"He drives a Maserati," I said.

"Same shit. Let's go to Maxine's."

❊   ❊   ❊

Greetz and I first met at a local screening room a few years
back. On the surface, we didn't figure; aesthetically, neither
of us belonged on the same end of town. Aside from a waning
interest in film—along with the nightly dram of grog—the
two of us shared almost nothing in common. For brethren
ilk, we were seldom mistook.

Tinsel—the Anarchist, Wonderboy, Fuck-O—the
Danish mother's outcast son of a Yankee insurance salesman
abroad, had grown up transient/semiprivileged (*gasp*)—although he'd never admit it—as part of a "white and worldly"
community, steeped in denial no less than security.

I, on the flip—the Half-Breed Rising, Hanoi Jackson,
Old Kim Crow—had been culled in numerous inner-city
foster homes for sixteen years, the orphaned son of a black
GI and (by report) a Cambodian prostitute—which, in the
era directly following U.S. involvement in Vietnam, en-
sured my part in NO COMMUNITY—black, yellow,
white or corn fed.

Both of us lived in the Desmon now, though for different, unrelated reasons—Tinsel with visions of starting a
movement, I by cause of my recent eviction.

Together we shared the distinction of being impossible
under conditions of peace.

Consequently, every time we got together, *something*
happened.

❋   ❋   ❋

We passed the afternoon at Maxine's, playing five-card stud with Money, the barman. Behind us, up on a stage, the Pine Street Blakes were hosting a poetry slam. The room was packed with gothic trash, everyone queued for a strike at the altar. Slowly but surely, the audience thinned as the day wore on. *Bleed it and leave . . .*

After a while, I ran my gaze across and over the seating area, past a table of heroin ghouls, between a frothing pusher and Money, along the opposite, moldering counter to numerous marks on the human condition—a jaundiced Feeder in detox, wheezing; an AWOL Ranger, passed out cold; someone's attempt at Nosferatu—filed fangs and implanted horns; a pair of hookers consulting the tarot; another ghoul with a skin condition; a tramp named Coley wrecked on glue . . .

How could this place, these *people*, have happened?

Pete came in. As Tinsel coined him: Pete McDermott, the Doper's Fiend—presently due in court for robbing a Girl Scout's lemonade stand on Spruce—along with his wife, Eliza Beth, an Iowa princess gone to smack; both of a certain age and fading, who funded their blight via whatever means, she by stripping, he by returning stolen goods to their point of purchase or, as appeared the case today, carting them all over Glokland Row.

"Last week he sold me *The Will to Power* for fifty cents," said Greetz. "Hey! McDermott!"

Pete looked up.

Tinsel beckoned. "Come over here!"

Pete came over, schlepping his load. " Hey,Tinsel!"

"Hey, yourself. This is Charlie."

"Hello, Charlie."

Money appeared. "You want something, Pete?"

"Yeah," flashing a torn dollar bill. "You got any tape?"

"Sure." Money produced a roll.

"Thanks," said Pete, then mended the bill—explaining how Eliza Beth threw him only her damaged money any-more. "Aw, Tinsel," he groaned from the pit of his clogged esophagus. "These jokers at the bar tear the dollars in half so they can cop twice the feel. Geez, I'll tell ya . . ."

"That's awful," said Greetz. "What's in the bag?"

"Records and stuff. Have a look."

Tinsel went through it, picking and sifting. He stopped. "Christmas." Pulled out a bullhorn. "*Tell* me this works."

"I think so," Pete said. "Go on. Try it."

Behind us, an angry young woman was nailing a pickle to the wall with a timber spike. "You're NOT MY FA-THER!" she screamed, then stormed offstage and locked herself in the can.

The crowd sat leveled. Grown men wept. The NEA was somehow to blame.

Tinsel flipped on the bullhorn, leveled it. "SHOW US YOUR TITS!"—with a roar.

They booed.

*

Money came over: "Cut it out, Greetz!"

"Right," said Tinsel, turning to Pete: "How much you want for this thing?"

"Fifty?"

"Go twenty?"

"Oh my God . . ."

"That's right. Twenty. Or *thirty* tomorrow."

"Twenty now."

"Settled. Give us a couple of minutes." Grabbing my arm: "Come on, Chuck!"

*   *   *

An hour later, Danny Gill, the area's champion lush, went down. Thereby, with scarcely a *cut* of the winner's take — but plenty of booze on my breath — I set out in search of a job. I found one: stocking beer at the corner deli. The boss, a flaming Dutchman, Hanz, regarded my every move with suspicion. However, at ten, he bade me leave — and even allotted me basic credit. I went home, back to the Desmon, hauling a case of domestic Black & Tan. Lulled to boredom by NPR, I fell asleep sometime after four.

*   *   *

In the months to come, my life in music would steadily fade to a distant memory — one defined by a blot of poorly managed and often booze-addled episodes. In their place would emerge a blurred succession of shifts at Hanz's "Swillery," many defined by a blot of poorly managed and often booze-addled episodes. Proofreading scores for the Philtharmonic would lead into stocking crates at the deli with relative ease and lesser adjustment, aside from a twenty-grand cut in pay. Likewise, relocating from Second and Cherry Streets to Glokland Row would entail a change of scenery over lifestyle—*that* much tends to linger: out of my insular, cobblestone cloud to the greater sprawl of urban decay with nary a cocktail party, banquet or dining affair to be lost in between.

TINSEL

In mid-December, Tinsel announced his latest scheme: the Barter System. Tinsel's Provisional Barter System: Rising Hope of the Urban Socialist. Months of work had gone into the title, and Greetz had spared no effort coining it. Back in October, he'd left for the Farm, a Mutualist compound in Oklahoma where "volunteers" explored the tenets of "modern alternative social reform." This entailed meeting with prominent "gurus" and plowing through stacks of leftist quarterlies—all in hopes of devising a plan, one to be tried on the ranks back home. Of course, its agenda was inexplicit. However, I gathered, the key lay in Marx . . . *Das Kapital*, the *Steal This Book* of 1880s, was Tinsel's scripture—even though his own edition, the one he flaunted as some kind of lost, unheralded revelation, per se, had been dog-eared on page seven and looked to be not three days off the shelf it was stolen from . . .

*

Foxhole Revolution Blues, take thirty.

In typical form, Tinsel hadn't gone beyond, or even *into*, basic theory. He didn't know the first thing about economics. He didn't know a Mutualist from a Sandinista. He couldn't *pronounce* half the titles he was citing. And his fabled compound was no doubt a squat full of hash-addled Okie Utopian Jive.

I could see them out there, ten or twelve sick types huddled in a wood shack, railing the system . . .

Greetz had returned to Philth Town promising brave new worlds in the season to come. For days he raved about founding a network of local craftsmen, all volunteers, among whom a free exchange of services might be conducted on a credit system — itself to be gauged and overseen through the distribution of credit slips. For example, a carpenter might be asked to repair another participant's woodwork — a task demanding nineteen hours of labor and, therefore, fetching two slips. That carpenter might then use those slips toward hiring a landscaping team for the day. One good turn would deserve another, in theory . . .

Or so the Anarchist claimed.

Right from the start, he knew *my* take: his plan was a bust, it would never fly — partly due to the void distinction between his slips and cold hard cash, but mostly in light of the *people* concerned: these thieving scrubs wouldn't last a day. They'd screw one another, then blame it on Greetz. Sure as rain, I told him so . . .

＊

Which, of course, only encouraged him. "Bonaparte had his skeptics, too!" he announced. "And who got the last laugh *there*?"

"Exactly!" I countered. "Wellington!"

"No, I mean — *before* that!" Scowling. "Smart-ass. Just you wait . . ."

Whereupon I dropped it.

In general, the longer you reasoned with Greetz, the more it inflamed his delusions of grandeur. Several examples come to mind —*far* too many—from over the years. When cautioned re: hosing his boss at the stockyards, he wound up slapped with a federal fine. When warned about planting a shit bomb in the post office, the box went off in his face prematurely. When urged not to streak through the park at dawn, he still got his ass kicked and three days in jail. And while coasting a dock cart into the river, against my advice, he bailed too late . . .

So when it came to the Barter System, his magnum opus, there was no point in arguing. All you could do was sit back and wait. This, and more, would come to pass.

＊ ＊ ＊

January opened with a record-breaking cold front. Everyone in town was forced indoors. Tinsel took advantage of the lull by wandering the hotel, drumming up local support. Soon he'd hustled a sizable crowd into giving his Barter System a shot. He'd even persuaded Jones to lend him the downstairs lounge for an opening meeting.

*

I, for one, remained out of the picture. I *did*, however, catch sight of that meeting. While crossing the lobby, I heard, then *saw* it: Tinsel looming in the doorway, back turned, blasting legal tender a capitalist ploy—a throng of crusties squatted around him, nudging and poking one another distractedly—a fuming pit of leather and dreadlocks cut with the tang of patchouli and foot rot . . . At first it seemed that I'd wandered into a casting call for *Satyricon*. With a closer look, perhaps the *Inferno* . . . I could not *believe* some of Tinsel's choices . . . Foremost being Hershell and the Sleestacks, that gang of housepainting Rastafarians widely renowned for crashing parties and sacking every flat they entered . . . Next, a coven of militant vegans from Baltimore Avenue's Organic Grain Shack, parked on the couch twirling their crystals, clearly appalled by the rash of carnivores . . . Then, numerous heroin ghouls, a veterinarian, somebody's *grandmother*—along with a couple of failed musicians, would've-been rockers and aging groupies . . . And finally, by far the clot in the whirl, the one that threw me over the railing: Dojo the Sumo Nazi—a gun-dealing, number-running, neo-blackshirt ivory merchant who kept the crowd in attendance stocked, if not dependent, on pharmaceuticals—everything from heisted quinine and novocaine to suppositories for heifers with gout . . . Technically speaking, Dojo *was* a certified plumber, though that only served to bolster his all too frequent claims of having the means and wherewithal to spike the city water supply with enough Jacob's Ladder to turn the streets into a free-form carnival of pilfering and brutality . . .

* * *

Needless to say, the project bombed. Straight to hell in record time. Truly, its failure was *so* complete that even *I* was caught off guard . . .

Right away, first thing in the morning—not *twelve* hours after the meeting was called—everyone present, including Tinsel, flocked to the Grain Shack to plunder house.

The Grain Wenches spent all afternoon on a frenzied public section eight—running to market, fighting with customers, furiously squabbling to and fro. By early evening, the kitchen staff had been jarred to the brink of collective meltdown. The servers and cashiers followed suit, careening through mounds of toppled crockery—everyone plastered in oil and cabbage with chunks of tofu knotting their hair. Based on subsequent word of mouth, it was *the* definitive antishift.

All eight of the Sleestacks were there for breakfast, lunch and dinner. Some of them brought their families along, insisting their credit included their kin. By seven o'clock, they were plastered on mezcal and homegrown dirt weed— *completely* out of hand: banging on tables, hollering for service, goosing the Wenches, flinging potatoes . . .

At last a cook ordered everyone out, at which point Hershell took a swing. The ensuing battle wound up in the street, where the cook was beaten and locked in a Dumpster. The Sleestacks, along with their friends and family, fled the scene in two separate camper vans.

*

Once the Shack was closed for the evening, the Wenches exhaustedly tallied their losses. The shelves were bare. The kitchen was wrecked. The freezer, empty. Furniture gone. There were missing lightbulbs, ashtrays, lamps, busted chairs all over the floor. A soiled diaper crammed in the radiator, bean curd smeared on the ceiling panels.

The staff was irate.

All nine of them had just undergone the most excruciating barrage of public abuse, stock theft and property damage in the Shack's history, yet the final count on the register wouldn't cover basic *power* expenses for the afternoon.

I was sitting with Greetz when his phone started ringing like ten thousand atom bombs trying to get through. He picked up the line. Voices boomed. Cringing, he held the receiver away. The voices continued, squawking and tearing. From where I sat, just one line was clear: "THIS WASN'T SUPPOSED TO BE THE IDEA!"

Tinsel, horrified, leaned on his desktop, frantically seeking a chance to interject. "Wait . . . wait a second . . . Hold on!" he pleaded, intermittently cupping the receiver to shoot me desperate, imploring looks. "Hold on there . . . but just . . ." — (*Shit, Charlie!*) — "just . . . please, just a . . ." — (*They're out of their minds!*) — "just . . . HOLD ON A SECOND!"

With that, they allowed him a word on the matter. He summoned his cool, then set about explaining how — although, okay, yes, so it *had* been one hell of a bad day, no argument there — if the Shack staff would just keep it together, they'd soon understand: this wasn't so bad. After all, they were now in possession of forty credit slips, right? Meaning: they were legitimately entitled to mass renovations, free of charge. They could get a coat of paint for the dining hall. They could retile the kitchen floor. They could overhaul the entire plumbing network, if need be. Whatever . . .

Slowly, the squawking simmered down. It leveled off to a hostile groan. Then fizzled out.

Greetz hung up.

He turned to me, trembling. We stared at each other. I held up my hands, real laissez-faire . . . He snarled anyway, lifting a finger: "Don't you say a goddamn word."

❉ ❉ ❉

So the Shack staff, heeding his advice, struck back. The Sleestacks, minus Hershell, were called in to paint the main floor. Dojo was contracted for general repairs in the kitchen, and Sam Hannah, the independent carpenter and onetime Amway rep, was summoned to restore four antique bureaus in the cellar. The Grain Wenches put them all to work and monitored their performances closely.

But pretty soon that fell apart, too.

For one thing, the Sleestacks couldn't very well paint the dining hall during business hours, yet the Grain Wenches wouldn't even *consider* leaving them the keys overnight . . . Right from the start, the situation was charged with resentment, scorn and mistrust. The Sleestacks, it was decided, were performing a deliberately third-rate job, and everyone involved seemed to share in the blame. Dojo returned to the Desmon one night complaining of "those tyrannical vegans."

"All I ever wanted to do was run dope!" he moaned. "Why won't they leave me alone?"

Even Sam Hannah was losing patience — "carnal discrimination," he called it. No one could take much more of this. In effect, the crew had been ordered to pull out a rigorous, forty-hour workweek in exchange for having eaten two or three bean burgers on a Saturday afternoon . . . (?) . . . Somehow, the trade didn't balance out.

Tensions came to a head on Wednesday morning, when two cashiers announced that the till had been robbed and that someone'd better come clean, *or else* . . . Dojo threw up his hands and walked out, soon to be followed by Sam Hannah. The Sleestacks, however, lingered on, feigning ignorance, even sympathy . . . One of them claimed to have spotted Hannah eyeing the till a few hours back and was now, come to think of it, *positive* he'd been up to no good . . .

The Wenches took the bait. The Sleestacks blinked. A cop came by to file a report.

Afterward things settled down for a bit. Reconciliation in the face of adversity. With shysters and criminals out of the mix, relations were cleared to proceed unhindered.

The next few hours went smoothly enough. By closing time, all was harmonious. Thereby, the staff agreed to leave the Sleestacks a set of keys for the evening in hopes that the dining hall might be completed in a single seven-hour sweep. Closing the kitchen in decent spirits, the cooks suggested a weekend party. Agreeing, the Wenches locked their till and, bidding the crew farewell, went home.

*   *   *

I'm glad I wasn't around when the phone started ringing the next morning. It was bad enough hearing everything later. . . .

I got home from work to find Greetz in my room (his was now "unsafe," evidently), storming circles around the bed, cursing and yelling, fit to be tied. I slunk in, dropped my bag on the desk, cracked a bottle of Black & Tan, did my best to stall the inevitable, then broke down and asked what was wrong.

It came in spurts, fleeting clarity choked in static, running as follows:

First, the Wenches had returned to the Shack that morning to find it blown for a whirl. Gallons of paint had been tossed on the walls. Furniture smashed, the till stomped to pieces, the kitchen sink shat in, both doors open and the Sleestacks, damn them, nowhere around. The entire building was in shambles; in the course of one week, it had been reduced to an open-air crack house — and it was all, every bit of it, *Tinsel's fault* . . .

Second, in then trying to contact the Sleestacks, he discovered that most of them had given false addresses and telephone numbers. He was able to reach only one, who, after a strained exchange, replied: "Ya, mon — toss off, I's quit . . ." Tinsel had then gone upstairs to speak with Hershell, only to find that Hershell had checked out of the Desmon two days earlier and left no forwarding number. His room was now occupied by an Irish transsexual in a mud mask.

Third, both Dojo and Sam Hannah had jumped ship as well—Dojo, on his end, claiming to have no more time for this madness and to never really having understood it in the first place . . . But with Hannah it wasn't so easy, as Hannah had spent the evening in central booking on robbery charges. He hadn't been released until nine that morning, upon which he'd marched straight to the Desmon, summoned Tinsel to the lobby and punched him in the gut.

And four, Sylvia, the group's token veterinarian, who, it now came out, had signed on only as a symbolic gesture, phoned to complain that she'd been overrun with demands to watch over numerous house pets. Six dogs had been left on her doorstep the very first morning. It was out of the question, she said. She was a *certified professional,* not a neighborhood dog-sitter. She was giving Tinsel exactly forty-eight hours to resolve this matter before she drove over and dumped the whole pack in the lobby herself . . .

And there were other details, but pretty soon Greetz spiraled into a blathering fit and I lost my bearings. At some point, I picked up a fleeting reference to Armless Rob and Xerox demands, something else about cooks and Grain Wenches threatening legal retaliation . . . But other than that, I had no idea. Tinsel was out of his fucking mind—stomping violently, flailing his arms, shrieking that only five days had passed, yet he'd already lost a knight, a bishop, and most of his pawns, and that all of these self-proclaimed insurgents, with all of their talk of direct action, and all of their calls for being honest in order to live outside of the law were, in truth, a horde of thieving, dishonorable, treacherous snakes, and to hell with them all . . .

❊ ❊ ❊

On Friday morning he started west. There was much to be done in little time. He had to *secure* an advance from Welsh's Tavern—the bar where he played his weekly gig—to *buy* paint to *repair* what was left of the Shack, come what may . . .

He was gone by seven-thirty.

Originally, I never intended to follow. The last thing I had planned for my day off was repair work at the Grain Shack. However, by noon the Desmon had roared to life, and quickly, my options were narrowed.

Across the hall, some ghouls had cornered a rat in the toilet and were calling for backup. Down in the street, a construction crew was slamming the pavement to ribbons *again*. Two doors over, Yancey had a stockbroker bound to the rack and braying like an ass. And just overhead, someone was throwing a ten-man YES party, stomping up and down . . . It was unendurable. I *had* to get out.

Which then left me wandering Glokland Row without so much as a dime to my name. That's when I started thinking of Tinsel—alone out there. Mired in the shit. *With*, at least, a roof overhead . . .

It seemed that I ought to go pay him a visit.

❊ ❊ ❊

From a block in the distance, I spotted the CLOSED FOR RE-PAIRS sign hanging above the doorway. I crossed the street beyond a sprawling line of rot and approached the window.

I cupped my hand to shield the glare for a look inside, into
the darkness . . . After a minute of probing the wreckage, I
spotted Tinsel — back in a corner — trying to spackle a strip
of molding. I tapped on the glass. He snapped to attention.
It took some time for my number to register. Then, relieved,
he dropped his knife and climbed over a pile of draped ob-
jects, tables and chairs, heaped up at mid-floor.

The door came open.

"Are you alone?" I asked.

"Yeah!" He spat on the mat, livid. "Damn hippies didn't
even want to *watch*."

"Do you mind if I come in?"

"Please do."

I had to straddle a mound of trash in the doorway before I could look around. By then I'd been hearing about
the Grain Shack for days. But *nothing* could've prepared me
for the actual state of it. The damage had to speak for itself . . . On every side, in bleak excess: holes in the wall,
wires dangling, smashed pottery across the floor — racks
overturned, busted lightbulbs, the bathroom and kitchen in
disassembly. And Tinsel there in the middle of it all — streaked
with paint from head to toe, wheezing, one of his eyelids
clotted — fully expected to fix *everything*.

He'd had one hell of a morning.

First off, Welsh's was none too thrilled about advancing him what amounted to eight nights' worth of wages. He
would have to play free gigs for the next month just to settle
up. And that being his *only* source of income.

Second, he'd then bought the wrong shade of paint from Sherwin-Williams, which meant he would now have to redo *all* the walls, even the spreads that were left undamaged.

Third, it turned out that one of the Grain Wenches had contacted a brother of hers from Brooklyn, so that, shortly after Tinsel's arrival, five steroid-fueled Italians appeared at the door with clear intentions of pounding him flat. He'd had to do some *fast* talking. Which worked, amazingly. I don't know how, but he *did* it—actually convinced them that he, the Anarchist, wasn't to blame—it was really those Sleestacks, those shit-eating Rastafarian ingrates and no one else. The Italians wavered, grumbling uncertainly, but when Greetz started doling out names and the one legitimate phone number from his notebook, they agreed to let him off, for the moment . . . They tooled away in an overburdened Subaru, promising return if his leads weren't valid.

And finally, once squared away in the shop, he wound up faced with the task at hand . . . He knew nothing about plumbing. He couldn't have spackled his way out of a cardboard box. He didn't know a drainpipe from a hole in the wall. He was completely fucked. All he could do was start painting, and judging by the look of it, *that* was out, too . . .

He was crazed. Traipsing around with a paint-flecked cigarette hanging from his lip. "Look at this shit!" He kicked the wall. "I just can't *believe* it."

A dishpan fell from a rack in the kitchen. Droves of mice shot over the floor. Tinsel grimaced, spitting again. "What the hell is *wrong* with these people?"

❁

He waxed schizophrenic for twenty-five minutes. In all that time, I didn't say a word. The only thing that (eventually) prompted me to get up and help was the onset of hypothermia. The Grain Wenches hadn't left the heat on. It was getting colder by the minute. Tinsel's winter jacket by now was soaked to the inner lining with paint. It was starting to crackle. His hands were blue. He looked like he'd been hit by a milk bomb.

"All right!" he yelled as I got to my feet. "I knew I could count on you, Chuck! We'll bang it out together. No problem. Come on!"

But the first thing he did was gut the wall, attempting to work a wire loose. A slide of plaster filled the sink. A cloud of it wafted over his head. He staggered back, blinded, choking, swinging the hammer in wild arcs. Edging away, I drifted into the dining hall to wait out the rampage . . .

When, at length, his voice returned, he flew off the handle, spewing invective. After a while, it got so bad that I left the shack altogether, disgusted.

I walked a block to the General Repair, bought a few rolls of paper and tape. Yet when I returned, he was *still* at it—shit, fuck and piss on *everything*. I had to land him a backhand to ward off the seizure. "Get it together!" I yelled.

He came around, spluttering, wide-eyed. "Okay. I'm here. I'm calm. All right . . . So, what?"

We started with the walls.

✳

I stuffed rags and towels into every hole. Then I cordoned them off with tape. Next I tried to smooth out the edges. But some of the patches began to sag. I had to remove whole strips for repacking.

Tinsel didn't understand. "What are you *doing*?"

"Just shut up and start wallpapering!" I snapped.

He opened a roll, regarded the print. "What is this?" He drew back. "*Donald Duck*?"

"We'll paint over it," I said. "You only had ten dollars left in the bucket."

"But Charlie—this isn't even wallpaper. It's *gift wrap*!"

"Just do it!" I hissed. "It can't get worse!"

He rolled out the paper, cut three strips. Coated one wall with a layer of glue, then positioned the first strip vertically. It wound up crooked and ripped with oblong pockets of air trapped under the surface. He did his best to iron them out but succeeded only in smearing more glue.

"It's not *working*!" he cried.

"Hold steady!"

He continued, tight-lipped, layering each wall. The gift wrap clung like soggy tissue. In time, he gave up on aligning the edges and simply lay down patches at random . . .

I was grappling with a hole above the sink, trying to plug it with a torn bedsheet. The wall kept falling apart in chunks. It was impossible. I got a piece of tape in place, but it soon gave out, dumping the sheet back into the sink with another cloud of plaster. I started over, eventually got it *half* secured . . . It looked like a flight bag jammed in the wall. Tinsel papered over it, groaning miserably.

I went to the john for a damage estimate. Didn't seem *too* bad . . . I called in Greetz. We lifted a sink from a box in the corner and attempted to mount it. But we couldn't . . . get . . . situated . . . "HOLD STILL!" I yelled, trying to connect a pipe with the basin's underside. Tinsel strained to hold it upright — one foot on the toilet, the other wobbling. He started to lose it. "No, *NO!*" The sink hit the floor and smashed to pieces. "**NO GOD SHIT FUCKER!**"

Some societies still drown their invalids at birth. Here we're left to do *ourselves* in.

"All right, all right — forget the sink!" Tinsel turned away from the heap of porcelain. "We can blame that on Dojo . . . Let's just get this place painted and split before those Italians come back."

I grabbed my brush. We started painting. Soon, Tinsel kicked the can. Sherwin-Williams all over the floor . . . He screamed, got down on all fours started scooping up paint with his bare, chapped hands. He dumped what he was able to gather back into the can. The rest soaked into the floor. Our remaining supply was tainted brown. He swirled it around. "There's not enough left!"

"Well, thin it down!"

He poured *way* too much turpentine in the can. "Aw, Charlie! What have I done?"

"Drain some off the top! Hurry!"

He ran to the sink, did his best. But it was still no good. Not even *close* — we were left with less than half a gallon of diluted mud for the entire level.

We started painting once more. It went on like pond murk — scum and hair curling out from the wall. Our base wasn't thick enough to cover the gift wrap. The room would need at least one more coat. And we were out of money, for *real* this time . . .

Our battle was lost halfway through the hall.

Tinsel dropped his brush on the floor. We looked around . . .

It was criminal. Atrocious. Whole *empires* had fallen to less ruin . . . Every wall a gutted collage of filth, potting glue, tape and gift wrap. The kitchen sink full of plaster and shit. Paint tracked over every inch of the floor. The bathroom wrecked. Mice everywhere . . . We had done more damage trying to *save* this place than the Sleestacks had in attempting to level it.

In the end, all Tinsel could summon was: "They're gonna sue the *shit* out of me."

I could only agree: he'd be lucky if the cops got to him before the Italians.

He turned around, a being broken. "Let's get out of here," he sighed. "Come on."

❧   ❧   ❧

Back at the Desmon, he was inconsolable. Didn't say a word, didn't even want to *drink*... Just—sat with his vacant, thousand-yard stare transfixed to the print of Ned Kelly on my wall...

That prior retort—the one about Bonaparte's skeptics—suddenly came to mind...

The fact is: at twenty-six, Napoleon had been at the head of an army, marching on Italy. Greetz, at the same age, couldn't handle a small posse of Bottom-feeders.

*   *   *

One room over, some kind of hate fest was rocking the walls of Emmy Lou's dungeon. Banging, wheezing, speaking in tongues. It sounded like a scene from *The Exorcist*. Horrible...

"You know," I suggested, "maybe you ought to pay her a visit later on. Might do you some good."

He peered around. "Who—the *yeti*?"

I shrugged. "Hey—she's not *that* bad..."

He stared.

"All right," I said. "Forget it."

He went back to picking paint from his hair—waiting for the next, yet one more, disaster.

And it wasn't long in coming.

We were drifting through a dead spell, contemplating silence (the antics next door had just tapered off)—both of us staring at Ned by then—when chaos erupted in the lobby downstairs. Followed by Jones howling upward. "GREETZ! EVANS! GET DOWN HERE! NOW!" We opened the door. A schnauzer ran by. Yancey Fishnet screamed in the can. Tinsel yelled something about forgetting Sylvia, not having known it would come to this . . .

Moments later, we reached the lobby to find a pack of dogs on the loose: rottweilers, tick hounds, shepherds, pit bulls climbing the walls in a scrambling rush—snooping through closets, lifting their legs, one of them humping Jones's thigh—others accosting ghouls in the lounge, the rest spreading panic and terror through the building.

"What *is* this?" Jones demanded, horrified.

I tried to squeeze out some explanation while Tinsel bolted to round up the pack. Jones cut me off in mid-harangue. "I don't care *where* they came from—just *get them out of here*! And take *him* with you!

Just then Armless Rob appeared. He was blown off his feet by a border collie. One sorry item, that: Braque portrait downed by rogue Lassie. I yanked it away, then extended one hand to Rob.

"What am I supposed to do with *that*?" he hissed.

Whoops.

He groped to his feet, pissed as hell. "Thanks a lot, Charlie!"—then traipsed away.

Tinsel facing the music upstairs. From two floors down, it sounded awful.

"Get outta here, you fuckin' idiot! Go back to Oklahoma!"

Restraining several dogs at once, he reappeared, stumbling downward. Disgusted, Jones threw us a rope. I set to work securing a harness. Tinsel split to round up the rest, huffing and schlepping his way through Our Lady . . .

It took some time to retrieve them all and a good while longer to knot the leash, by the end of which a crowd had gathered to rail us both as despicable assholes.

❊   ❊   ❊

The last I saw of Greetz that night, he was plodding into the arctic death with eleven baying dogs in tow, straining and lurching in every direction . . .

Across the river, he set them free in an all-night Wawa and ran like hell. But with nowhere to go from there, he was forced to turn to his ex, Zelda, whom he'd left for a stripper six months earlier . . .

I don't know why she let him back in.

BEN

Every winter, the sewage-treatment plant, Botgwanow's, Inc., sent manual exterminators or, loosely, "slaghands," into the sewers on rodent detail. These forays were known as the Willard Rounds. Their basic function ran as such:

With underground tunnels throughout fast-food strips emanating heat and organic aromas, several zones were infested with rats, *unmanageably* so, by year's end. Initiating standard "cleansing" procedures without first thinning the ranks otherwise might prove not only ineffective but possibly a public threat, i.e., an exodus of crippled scavengers from out of the sewers and into the streets. This "Ben Stampede" would favor no one, least of all the treatment plant.

With that in mind, Botgwanow's itself made an earnest, though not altogether *legal,* attempt to resolve the matter by posting labor calls in flophouses all through the city. Places like the Desmon were targeted foremost. Tenants therein leapt to the call.

As with the Feeders, though one step *beyond*, most slag-hands lingered just off of skid row. They were living wrecks by nature and requirement. The Willard Rounds took a special breed . . .

—Who else would engage in this backdoor racket in spite of a ban by the EPA?

—Who would traverse a river of shit with no proper training or health insurance?

—Who else would risk getting lost in a submain, blown off his feet by disposal blasts, burned to a crisp in a methane explosion or killed and devoured by ten thousand rats?

Indeed, the job was a full-bore nightmare—unquestionably the foulest labor in town. The only incentive, of course, was the pay, which topped the bracket, by Kulak standards. You received $90 for meeting a quota (usually forty to fifty rats) and $1 for every three thereafter. Not so bad, when you did the math. Most slaghands could meet the quota in an hour, leaving the rest to capital gain. On a good day, you might even net two bills. But you broke your back for every penny.

❃   ❃   ❃

I got wind of these operations three months into my stay at the Desmon. By then, Feeders all over the building were coming home rich, though exhausted, each night. I'd spot them drinking good Scotch in the lounge and, not knowing better, wonder how. Eventually, somebody clued me in . . .

Shortly thereafter, I joined the crew.

❋

At that point, all of my energies were geared toward leaving the city, for*ever*, if possible. Now that my gig with the union was shot, nothing remained to keep me around. Finding "wealth in poverty" here, on Glokland Row, was out of the question. Besides, for years, not a day had gone by when I hadn't dreamed of splitting town . . .

As for destinations, there were none. I wasn't intent on a promised land. I didn't envision bottles of wine in Italian courtyards or nights in Tangiers.

True, I'd ruled out heading south. Visions of Texas got in the way. The Half-breed thumbing his way through the panhandle?

Thank you, no. To hell with the Lone Star.

But all the rest was fun games. Delis across the planet hired. Ghanzi, Botswana, or Dale, Indiana — it made no difference. The grass *was* greener.

❋   ❋   ❋

I pulled my first round just before Christmas. It paid out $180. Back upstairs, I returned to the grind with a whole new take on sweatshop labor.

Two weeks later, I went down again. The second round was more lucrative yet. Much as I hate to admit it now, I was good at the job — some said a natural.

Typical, that: leave Chuck to his field as a "seasoned pro" and he's not worth a damn, but throw him to Ben for an afternoon and he's right at home, king of midnight.

✿

By halfway through January — moving on — I'd managed to stash over $400. I might've departed on that much alone, but to *stay* gone, I figured, a grand was in order.

I waited around, working the deli, skimming its till every chance I got . . .

Then, unexpectedly, word let out that Sector Six was to be reopened.

✿   ✿   ✿

Sector Six, or Dead Man's Lair, was a network of storm sewers spanning south Philth Town. The zone had been ruled off-limits in Gipper Time, following a slaghand's sudden disappearance. The department then sealed the perimeter indefinitely. No one had probed it since '87. To all but a handful of veteran Feeders, Dead Man's Lair was an urban myth. Beyond speculation, just one thing was certain: after so many years of neglected control, the district was sure to be teeming with quarry. Hence, the allure of Botgwanow's announcement.

The coming round would stand apart in that Tinsel would now be along for the ride. Try as I had to find *some* other partner, none was available. Prospects accounted for. Only the Anarchist, shacked up at Zelda's with no steady income, could heed the call.

✿   ✿   ✿

Greetz hadn't held down a straight job in years. He had no presentable résumé to speak of. He'd blown most gigs before receiving a paycheck, and lost the others in under a month. Excepting a cut from his draftsman's commission (proofreading Danish tourist brochures), he hadn't been taxed since the age of twenty-two. The IRS barely knew he existed. Of late, employers responded thus: "We're sorry, Mr. Greetz —while your dossier *does* look promising, and we *are* currently expanding operations, one too many questions has been raised regarding the evident gaps in your employment record —as in, namely: *where have you been for the last forty-nine months*?"

Whereupon Tinsel would draw up a comeback, claiming —"funny you should ask"—he'd been holed up with the Piggly Wiggly assistant manager's mail-order bride on the outskirts of Schnookumsville, nursing a dose of the Blue Ridge Molluscum brought home from Lana Turner's boar farm . . .

He'd spend whole days drafting each letter, figuring once his "case" had been made, they'd hire him in a flash, sheerly by virtue of his undeniably dazzling wit . . .

Needless to say, none of it worked. As far as I know, he *never* got a callback —an outcome he attributed wholly to the "sheer gullibility" of "bourgeois cave fish." He reckoned himself misunderstood: *far* too ahead of his time for the world. "They just don't get it!" he'd claim, half boasting. And verily, true—there was nothing to get.

In the end, having failed to provoke a response —*or* a psychiatric referral—he'd go on his way, cockstrong in exile, back to the taverns for another round of pub gigs.

Which was all good and well, until *those* ended, too.

❊

Since the demise of his Barter System, Greetz had been
hiding in Zelda's squat. With half of the neighborhood
out to kill him, he couldn't land a job, much less walk the
streets.

Although the Italians were back in Brooklyn and all five
Sleestacks holed up in jail, there was still a warrant for Tinsel's
arrest on four different charges, from dognapping to larceny.
In addition, Welsh's had canned him for failing to pay back
the Shack paint loan. Then he was spurned by the Jefferson
General, pronounced unfit for an upcoming drug study. Further, he'd OD'd on NyQuil, pushing a moderate cold to the
brink of pneumonia. And last, in the act of shoplifting *rice*, he
was spotted and flogged by Korean clerks . . .

After three weeks at close quarters with (*"all-she-wants-
to-do-is-fight!"*) Zelda, he'd *had* it. *Enough* . . . He was *sick to
death* of living like an animal. This lack of essentials was
doing him in. He *demanded* a space heater, blankets, tobacco,
corn chips, pocket change, dignity, booze . . . And he was
also making noise about needing a pistol . . . It was time, evidently, to *cut to the chase* — to hell with these piddly, *small-
change endeavors.* The day had come:

He was going to rob a bank.

"Check it out, Breed," he announced by phone, "all I
need's a gun and a getaway car . . ."

I hung up.

❊

Tinsel could blow his pay on funding a dwarf-throwing league, if he wanted. Our motives for detail were one and the $ame. After that, we parted ways.

❊ ❊ ❊

Since early autumn, a city crew had been uprooting Seminole block by block. Every morning at eight A.M., the jackhammers blew like a nuclear field test . . . Down in the street, car alarms activated, sirens let out, a generator boomed. Inside the Desmon, panic let loose: shouting, fighting, banging on walls . . .

For six weeks and running, this was what passed for a wake-up call in the House of the Damned. Monday morning was no exception.

Things would be different in Dale, Indiana.

I left the building at twenty past. A group of slaghands followed. Together, we cut through the trash lot. Then I split from the pack, moving west.

Sprawling ranges of ice and rock salt bracketed Dowler clear to the river. Most of the sidewalk was buried solid. Here and there, whole *cars* were entombed.

Once the roar of the hammers faded, the quarter was desolate. Every street lay quiet and empty. Even the rail yards were closed for the week.

I crossed the track bed, rounding a boxcar, and made my way down a gravel path. The Elm Street Bridge loomed up to my right. A flock of gulls spotted its railing. Beyond the opposite, vacant freeway, smokestacks rumbled, belching filth. A low-riding shelf of storm clouds hovered. I pushed through the weeds to an overgrown dock.

The river was frozen from bank to bank, with Greetz in between, spinning circles. Eight or nine flannels trailed from his back, an array of trash pocked the ice at his feet.

"Look at this, Chuck!" he called from below.

"Look at what?"

"The river," he said, "like a glass-bottom boat."

Yeah, I thought — *through a septic bayou . . .*

Leaning forward, he puffed on a smoke and peered through the ice for some sign of movement. "Man, I think there's a *car* down there." He pecked the surface, then: "Yeah, there *is*!"

"How can you tell?"

"Cuz," he muttered, "I'm reading the license . . ."

"The license."

"All right — not *quite* . . . But still, you can *see* it . . ."

"Be careful," I said. "Looks hairy down there."

"Bah!" Dismissing me. "Hairy, nothing." He pointed to the bridge. "Don't you remember? This is where Gerald botched the jump."

I followed his gaze. "What are you talking about?"

"Fat Gerald," he answered. "The cook at Lucille's. You heard that one, didn't you?"

"Yeah." I shrugged. "I heard about that. But I never actually thought it was true. It sounded like voodoo doll Melanie jive . . . And anyway, didn't that happen in Jersey?"

"Nope." He shook his head. "Happened right here. And it's *definitely* true. I've still got the article pinned to my wall."

*

I had to wonder which wall that meant . . .

He stooped to pick up a can from the ice. Thumbing the metal, he laughed out loud. "Gerald's all-time claim to shame: the only person in city history to botch an attempt from the Elm Street Bridge."

"Is that *really* what happened?" I asked, unconvinced.

"Yes." He nodded, along with an afterthought: "Only guy dumb enough to *try* it, too."

I considered the drop. "That's just the problem. It's *too* dumb. Really."

"There's no such thing." He slid to a spot between two columns. "You know *that*."

"All right," I conceded. "So what's the story?"

"The story is . . ." He pitched the can. It cleared the bridge and landed upriver. "Things had been going real bad for ol' Gerald. I guess he reckoned it time for the plunge. But the problem was—" He stomped on the ice. "This shit is *hard* when it freezes over. You could park a forklift out here no problem."

"You mean he actually *hit* the ice?"

"Damn straight. It's all on file. The papers compared it with diving headlong out a four-story window to solid concrete . . . Broken legs, busted ribs, a fractured skull— the works, *shattered* . . . — the fat's what saved him—held everything together like a hot sack of glue."

I shuddered. "*Jesus*."

"Aye, lad!" He choked back the pidgin Irish, holding steady. "But wait, there's more . . . When the rescue team finally arrived, a medic fell through the ice over there"—

pointing to a spot down below, on my left—"and wound up in critical for over a week . . . Now." He slipped into "clarity" mode. "*Now*—" he said it again for effect, "just how it is that four hundred pounds of that fat fuck spiraling out of the sky—fails to put even a *chip* in the ice, while his would-be savior, at *half* the weight, falls through on tiptoe not five yards from shore—well, as they say, it's *anyone's* guess. But that *is* what happened."

He dragged on his smoke. Then, forcing back laughter, he added: "The crew was so pissed off at Gerald, they sent him to jail. Not the hospital. *Jail.* And he stayed there all night. It's a wonder he made it."

"What was his problem?" I asked.

"Problem?"

"Why did he try to kill himself?"

"Oh, *that* . . . Well"—sighing—"the paper said he lost a bet and went on a drunk, or some such load. That's not what I heard."

"What did *you* hear?"

He flicked the butt. "I heard it was love."

"What did you say?"

"I said: it was *love.* His girlfriend left him."

I frowned. "Typical."

"*Typical* what?"

"Fat Gerald. Typical idiot."

"Well, *yeah*." He shrugged. "That's a given. But you can't say he didn't have a reason."

I stared.

Stopping, Tinsel looked up. "What?"—as though braced for the catch. Then: "What's this, now? *Cynical*, are we?" Grinning, he challenged: "All right then, you—let's have it, no jive: You couldn't see ending it for love?"

I waited. "What am I missing here?"

"Just *answer* the question."

"Okay. No."

"You *sure* about that?"

"*Yeah,* I'm sure."

He held his peace for a moment, then broke. "Shit!" He laughed. "And what kills me is you *believe* it, too! You're *hope*less, man."

I spread my arms.

He started toward me, shaking his head. "So just for the record—what *would* it take?"

Still confused: "To end it?"

"Yeah."

"Destitution?"

That really got him going. "But you *are* destitute, Charlie! Jesus."

"Speak for yourself. *I'm* not destitute . . ."

"No?" He balked.

"Not at all."

"Then why are you living in Our Lady Kettlehole?"

"Cuz—I'm broke. Not destitute. *Broke.*"

"I see." He reached the dock below. "And what, pray tell, is the difference, exactly?"

I thought it over, storming my options. "I don't know . . ."

What a question.

❄

He scaled the ladder, rose into view. "And the verdict?" he said. "Come on, let's have it!"

"Yeah, all right." I gave it a shot: "Broke's when you can't put food on the table."

"And destitute?"

"Means you can't afford booze." I turned to the rail yards, lighting a smoke of my own. "We're late," I said. "Let's go."

✽   ✽   ✽

For several streets surrounding Botgwanow's, the air hung thick with the stench of toxins. The building's interior was even worse; a lavender haze shrouded the floor. We stood between sludge tanks, randomly gagging through wafting clouds of stool and ammonia. Our ten-minute wait in the medical line was a training camp in nausea control.

Inside the office, a bowlegged nurse with crumbs in her mustache gave us the squeeze. Tinsel was ordered to drop his drawers for two different needles, one in each cheek. Next in line, a splotchy assistant presented us cups of yellow paste. Then we were shown to the dressing room, where two men in black stood doling out masks.

Tinsel examined his mouthpiece for blockage while I pulled our gear from a soiled hamper. Together, we found open lockers and stripped. The vinyl suits went on like armor ... Tinsel clipped his mask into place. I drew the zipper up my torso. We gathered our load sacks, lead pipes and lanterns, then made for the exit along with the others.

✽

Out in the yard, some trucks were parked at the base of an elevated storage tank. Several loaders were spaced in between, pitching bags of sand down the line. The slaghands stood in a clearing below, milling around the edge of a manhole. We moved to join them, trailing our sacks, yet two more grunts on scowry detail . . .

For the next few minutes, I did my best to caution Greetz as to what lay in store. I reckoned it fitting to stress certain hazards like slop blasts, methane and straying off course. I also intended to run through some chops, though clearly, my efforts were bound for naught.

"Save your breath!" He cut me off, turning away. "I know what I'm doing!"

Thereafter, watching him yak and prattle, I waited in silence till Dawson appeared.

Of six hundred staffers employed by the company, Francis Dawson was our only contact. Barring a handful of clerks and technicians, the rest of the department remained off camera. Dawson alone, all three hundred pounds of him, had been appointed to oversee detail. Whether that fact reflected his eminence or expendability we never knew. His bearing this morning suggested the latter, but after all, it was ten below . . .

*

Assuming position, he chattered his way through a round of precautions, point by point. Due to the sector in question, he said, the following measures were strongly advised: stick with our partners, forage slowly and never stray more than five yards from the trunk. Otherwise, nothing new to the drill: our lanterns were fitted with digital clocks that would sound automatically after six hours, whereupon we would return to base, tally our loads, get paid and leave.

He made a call for general questions, walked to the manhole and pulled back its cover. The rest of the slaghands filed into place, sealing their masks with a unified groan.

Tinsel and I were the last ones down, numbers twenty-one and -two. We lowered ourselves into the trench, let go of the ladder and backed away. The circle of light overhead closed off as the iron lid was dragged into place. The slaghands splashed away to both sides, leaving us solo in Dead Man's Lair.

Right from the start, it was plain to see: the only thing worse off than Glokland Row was the semi-elliptical trunk of its underside. All around us, in dank profusion: gurgling chutes, rotting mains, laterals gone, whole arches in ruin. The ceiling dense with bulbous cones of fecal matter, bacteria, scum. Tubes of asbestos cement interlocked with buckled pipes through worn lead fittings. And meandering west in a flat bottom trench, a steaming river of Philth Town disposal.

"My *God*, Charlie!" Tinsel groaned.

"Keep it down!"

"What?"

"Your *voice*!"

Slowly, I clipped the sack to my belt. Then I flicked on the portable lamp. Tinsel attempted to follow my lead but soon dropped his pipe in the slop. "Whoops!" He plunged after it, clear to an elbow, moaning and retching while probing the trench. "Fuck!" he choked. "This is disgusting!"

"There." I pointed. "Off to your left."

He shifted—"Ah!"—came up with the pipe. It was caked in ooze. He banged on the wall.

"Stop making noise!" I hissed. "Goddamn it!"

He jerked upright. "Sorry. Okay . . ." He lowered his pipe back into the current, scraping and dragging one end on the floor. "Don't mean to make such a racket," he muttered. "It's just that there's sludge on the knucklebar, dig?" He pulled up again. "There—better." Flicking his lamp: "Now—where to?"

I pointed. "That one."

We started forward, tracking west. A row of wall lamps lit the way. Overhead, ruptured check valves hissed, fogging the air with thick, milky vapors.

"It's hot down here!" Tinsel announced.

I was already sweating inside the plastic.

"Like traction!" he groaned. "Chafed ass!"

Again, I told him to shut his mouth.

We continued in silence. The tunnel was still. Only the slosh of our footsteps resounded. Inside the suit, my heartbeat pounded and boomed in time with every breath.

When a train rolled by somewhere in the distance, the current beneath us rippled and shook. A wave of patterns

crossed the ceiling. The shaft lights flickered, then caught
and held.

❊   ❊   ❊

A minute later, I killed the first rat. It shot from a valve box
into the slop. I tagged it clean. The walls were sprayed. The
impact tore through my forearms and triceps. Shifting position, I held out the lamp. The body surfaced. Gently, I
bagged it.

A few yards on, another appeared. The crack of lead
on bone filled the shaft.

Turning to Tinsel: "Think you can handle it?"

"Yeah. You want I should take the lead?"

"If you're ready, yes."

He sidled around me. I cut my lamp and followed along.

For the opening stretch, he seemed all right . . . A bit
awkward, of course, but nothing grievous. He kept it quiet,
shielded his lamp and moved with the current, just as I'd
shown him. On nearing a corner, he slowed to acknowledge
the squealing and rustling ahead, within earshot. I tapped
his shoulder, flashed a thumbs-up. He nodded, turned and
proceeded in silence.

We crept to the edge with our backs to the wall. Flex-
ing his grip, Tinsel halted. Then, in a flash, he rounded the
corner.

Sadly, that's where the hope ended.

Before I could move, he was flailing and whooping and
running amok on a psychotard spree. Crying for death at

the top of his lungs. Slamming his pipe on the wall and ceiling. Dropping the lamp, losing his balance, stumbling headlong into a switch box . . .

There could have been nothing less graceful about it.

Of the six or seven rats in view, he tagged only one, by sheer accident. And didn't kill it at that. *Or* stick around to finish the job . . . The rest got away by a long shot, gone. Tinsel went after them anyway, howling. The lone victim was left behind, writhing and twitching in tawny gristle. I finished it off with a blow to the skull, then dropped to my haunches to wait out the pause . . .

He was gone for a *ridiculously* long time. And when he *did* return, empty-handed of course, he was sporting an attitude, throwing off excuses. "I think there's something wrong with my pipe!" he (actually) attempted to claim. "I don't know what happened. Damn thing."

I looked at him.

"*What?*" He went on the defensive. "*Screw* you!"

I tossed him his rat, for all it was worth. "I can see I'm dealing with a natural here."

He dropped his pipe and punched the wall, railing me as black Cambodian trash. He almost looked ready to go right there. And I would've obliged, if not for the slop blast . . .

As though on cue (by order of decency), a tide of disposal blew from the wall. Tinsel was ripped off his feet in mid-sentence. He keeled over backward, thrashing. His head went under. The chute sprayed on. I turned away, unable to watch . . .

When it was over, he got to his feet, plastered in sewage from head to toe. His goggles were smeared with thick green discharge. Strands of bowl rot clung to both arms. The look on his face, obscured though it was, not hard to imagine: shock, *stupefaction* . . .

In just a few minutes, he'd kicked up a ruckus, been hit by a blast and taken the plunge—and through it all, counting the dead, had failed to deliver a single clean blow . . .

*   *   *

Two halls down, we passed a pair of slaghands. They loomed into view from a submain shaft. Their suits and gear were still fairly clean. Their sacks had begun to bulge with cargo . . . They looked us over, noting our loads and regarding Tinsel as some kind of beast. I wanted to stop and explain somehow but didn't get the chance—they passed without comment.

"All right," I decided once they'd gone. "We've got to do something here. This is embarrassing."

Tinsel shifted, raising his lantern. "How 'bout this way?" he said, pointing left.

"No, that's empty. *They* were just down there." I motioned ahead. "And that's shot, too. We're a long way off from anything, damn it."

"What about there?" He waved to the right.

I shook my head. "Off-limits. Forget it."

"What do you mean, 'off-limits'? Come on. I betcha it's packed."

"I'm sure it is. But that's how people get lost down here. These lateral shafts go on for miles. Without any lights, it's not worth the risk."

"Oh, come on!" he pleaded, determined. "We won't get lost. Let's just have a look."

I stared down the hall. Solid black . . .

The possibilities flashed before me.

On one hand, I pictured a miserable death in some uncharted shit mire, doom, entrapment . . .

But then I thought, *No* —a quick look around wouldn't do any harm, providing we're careful.

I finally spoke. "All right, listen. We'll give it a try. But *slowly.* Agreed?"

"Agreed." He nodded, lifting his sack. "I've just got to find my *chi,* that's all."

❖   ❖   ❖

Despite reduced visibility and clearance, he handled the next round in better form. His chops were clean; his collection, swift. Even his war cries were kept under wraps. The upgrade yielded a sizable batch. I followed along, more relieved than impressed.

By ten yards in, he was holding his own. I was ready to turn him loose and get going —this piddling around had cost me dear at the worst of times: opening hour. With everyone else razing the jackpot, I stood alone, bereft.

Knowing as much, we *had* done well by leaving the trunk as, despite all else, the shaft on hand was crawling with quarry from slop line to meter box. *Snakepit* dense.

Around the first corner, I kicked up a nest. Norway rats the size of possums — standing their ground, glistening, baleful. I had to move quickly to ward off attack . . .

During retrieval, a chill shot through me. I straightened up for a look around. The tunnel ahead, a sloping lateral, seemed to be humming with unseen movement. Visibility dimmed beyond a few yards. No sound was emitted, for all I could hear. But the *feeling* was there — something awful: a thousand eyes watching from all sides at once . . .

I backpedaled into the darkened submain. From there I could keep a lock on Greetz, the trunk shaft lights would remain in view. Yet even so, that chill persisted . . .

Hand over fist, the onslaught multiplied. Soon enough, we were hopelessly swamped. From out of the black, they advanced in waves, rolling along in black undulations . . . Moments earlier, pickings had lacked. Now it was all we could do to keep up. And as it continued, the outlook progressed from bad to bleak to fucking *impossible* . . . Soon, we were back to back at a standstill, furiously whacking and chopping at random, the current around us blossoming crimson, the shaft walls sopped in intestinal matter.

At some point, I knocked a rat from the ceiling. It fell to my head and clung on tight. Tinsel reacted, clubbing me sideways, then managed to cleave it in two on the drop. He followed up with an overhand swing, killing three more in a single blow, soon to be joined by a pair in the trench and, lastly, a loner in flight from above . . . And with that, I real-

ized, lo and behold, that Tinsel really *did* have the goods. Surprise, surprise. The Anarchist Greetz—a first-rate slaghand.
Who woulda thunk it?

Finally, a cease-fire. The horde retreated. We stood
there, wheezing, shin-deep in carnage.

Tinsel coughed. "We must've bagged the quota already."

"Yeah, it would seem." I peered around. "But I don't
understand this. I've never seen *anything* . . ."

"*Like* it?" he asked.

"Yeah." I nodded.

"Well, maybe the neighborhood changed this year. I
mean, maybe they added a factory or something. Where *are*
we, anyway?"

"Hard to say. Twenty-sixth and Barton?"

"*Twenty-sixth and Barton?*" He stiffened. "*Aawwgghh . . .*"
Gazing around. "That's the *garbage* strip, Breed! Joanie's.
Fuckin' *Blue Castle* . . . *I* don't even eat that shit!"

"I know. Watch your ankle." I pointed. "Got a live one."

He kicked without looking—"Filthy bastards!"—unhooked his pipe and swung with a holler.

"Did you get it?" I asked.

"Yeah." He spat. "Last time I *ever* do this, goddammit!"

We sloshed downstream to overtake the load. Along
the way, Tinsel spoke up. "Have you ever seen *C.H.U.D.*?"

"No," I said.

"Ah!" Relieved, he began to explain: "There's this species of nuclear sewer cannibals . . ."

A clang let out. I shot to attention.

A muffled rumble swelled through the tunnel.

Both of us froze, coiled to bolt at a moment's notice. The rumble intensified.

First, I assumed it was only a train—one with a damaged suspension or brake failure. But as it got louder, I moved on to *pigeons*—some underground flock in transit, roost-bound. Next, I thought about sinkholes, methane and, finally, *earthquake*—the big one, at last . . . By the time the rumble began to subside, I was all out of whack, at a stultified loss.

"What was *that*?" I hissed through the settling silence.

Tinsel backed off from the wall, trembling.

I plodded over. "Did you knock into something?"

"I think—" He held out his lantern. "*This* . . ."

An old iron door was set back in the stonework—rusted locks, a crumbling frame . . . It was some kind of switch room or transformer vault, though it obviously hadn't been used in years.

Snapping out of it, Tinsel blew: "Did you *hear* that, Chuck?" He shrank from the door. "There must be *thousands* of 'em! . . . Jesus fucking shit freak—*let's get out of here!* Come on! Let's *go*!"

"Wait!" I caught him by the arm. "Cool it!"

"*Cool it, my ass! We're in the middle of a Ben Lagoon!*"

"You sound like Michiko."

He stopped. "Like *who*?"

"Never mind. Just wait . . ."

I lifted my lantern to scan the wall. Four small holes to the left of the door, two at waist level, two up above . . . Otherwise, nothing. No way out.

"All right, we need some bricks," I whispered.

"What are you talking?" he blurted. "Fuck that! I told you I'm not staying down here."

"Look, *Greetz* — " I had to *not* yell. "If you do exactly as I say, we'll finish this job in the next ten minutes, then split forever. You got it?"

He stared.

"I'll take that as *yes*. Now fetch us some bricks!"

He traipsed off, seething, indignant, powerless. I heard him cursing around the corner. A minute later, he reappeared. "There!" — pitching two bricks in the slop.

"Find more," I said.

"To *hell* with you!"

I turned away. He splashed off again.

Quietly fishing each brick from the current, I managed to block the highest holes. The others, both on the level, were spaced out evenly, seven or eight feet apart.

Tinsel came back, toting more bricks.

"Okay," I said. "Now *you* keep one."

He passed me the other.

I turned, pointing. "Cover that end. You know what we're doing?"

"Yeah, I've got it!" He whirled, torn between rage and terror. "I still say it's crazy." He rolled up his bag. "But if we *must* . . ."

I sloshed to the vault, hung up my lantern.

This was it.

Gripping the pipe, I rolled my shoulders. Bashed the door.

*

The holes exploded.

Tinsel jammed his sack to the first, allowing Ben to spill right in. The other sprayed like a toxic geyser, hosing the opposite wall with quarry. I let it blow for several moments, kicking the slithering mass at my ankles. Then, moving on, I plugged the gap and flew into a slop-blind killing frenzy.

Most of the horde got away by a long shot. And the current took more than half our score. But we still made out like never before — Tinsel especially, sniveling bitch.

I turned to spot him sealing his hole with the last of our bricks. "Fucking *hell*!"

He hoisted the load sack over a shoulder, then slammed it against the wall repeatedly. The cargo inside squirmed and shrieked. Tinsel chimed in, retching obscenities. After a minute, he dropped the bag and beat the remaining life out of it.

He emerged with a catch already exceeding all but the load I was able to gather.

I sloshed to his side, wading through blood and innards. "You know," I said, wheezing. "For a lackey stooge, you're not doing badly."

"Yeah," he accepted. "But what does that *mean*?"

We stood there, reeling, speechless, astounded. Our load sacks bulged in the trench beneath us. We'd never be able to haul them to base without busting a seam, if not our backs. Sad to say, we'd been underequipped. Poorly accomodated. Short-sighted blind. The company couldn't provide for our type. As slaghands, we ranked unprecedented, *Godlike* . . .

The rest was simple — as Tinsel claimed: like gathering wild onions in a meadow.

I'd open a hole to let Ben make his break, then jam it shut and go to town. In three or four rounds, we were packed to the drawstrings. All that remained was a speedy retreat.

Back in the trunk, we found a ladder. I scaled the rungs to an iron lid. From there, I could make out the whine of traffic, chain-lined tires, a snowplow, engines . . .

I grabbed the lid and started to twist. It gave with ease. I pushed it up. It cracked out of sight. Tires on asphalt. Blaring. Screams.

Tinsel, confused: "What did you do?"

"A car hit the lid!" I yelled in a panic.

A face popped into view overhead — some toothless honky, throwing a fit. I started upward, *C.H.U.D.* reborn. He took one look and backed away . . .

I cleared the rim to find myself jamming a four-way intersection at (where else?) Twenty-sixth and Barton — exactly dead center between Joanie's and Blue Castle — with eight lanes of traffic backed up all around me, a terrified honky running scared and his car kicked sideways, engine stalled, at the end of a patch of smoldering rubber.

❋

Welcome back to life upstairs.

The honking and shouting welled to a peak as Tinsel
hoisted my sack from below. Somebody yelled that we ought
to be shot. A purple Toyota revved and bucked . . . By the
time our second bag had cleared, I was set to be clipped in
a hit-and-run.

I went to retrieve the upturned lid while Tinsel pulled
himself from the hole. Together, we managed to seal the
hatch and hustle our overstuffed loads to the curb.

Traffic resumed. Cars rolled by. Stiff middle fingers,
contempt, derision . . .

"You know," mumbled Greetz, shaking his head.
"People around here'd cut your throat for a quarter." He
paused to consider. Then, with conviction: "One of these
days this city'll burn."

❋   ❋   ❋

We headed south on Twenty-sixth, two roving slop mon-
sters, straight out of Valdez . . . Buses veered. A crack whore
swooned . . . You'd think we were doing something *illegal.*

Again, I pictured fleeing town. There was nowhere to
go, just plenty to leave.

We kept on, plowing our booty in starts—blood-coated,
shit-thrown, oozing putrefactive . . .

My bag broke open outside of a diner. Cross-eyed rats
all over the pavement. A line of faces gagging in the window. The cry of a terrified child within.

We dropped to our knees to clear the mess. A waiter appeared, gulping air. Someone threw us a sack from the kitchen. We tied up fast, then split, reviled.

Three alleys later, Greetz found a shopping cart—a mangled heap of wire with one leg missing. Tossing our sacks in its basket, we rolled away, bucking in starts.

❋ ❋ ❋

We got to Botgwanow's exactly one hour from the minute we'd left. Timing, that. The rest of the slaghands were just getting started. Tinsel and I were done for the season.

I banged on the door, then stepped aside, unhooked my mask and pulled back, gasping. A prickly chill shot over my scalp. Light, volume, wide-open air . . .

Dawson appeared a moment later, at first seeming angry to find us back early. Then he caught sight of our shopping cart. His expression dropped to utter astonishment.

We left him there to tally the load, adjourned to our lockers, stripped to the buck. A scalding-hot shower never felt any better; the cigarette afterward, downright sublime.

Back in the lobby by twenty past. The count came in a few minutes later. Still incredulous, Dawson appeared with a stack of money. We took it and walked.

CHARLIE

Greetz and I were leaving the liquor store, ending (his) five-hour shopping spree, when a weather flash came over the radio, discouraging all outdoor activity. By then the wind had picked up fourfold. The temperature was holding at thirty below. Braving the chill, we piled our loot in a taxi and rolled back to Zelda's squat.

After dinner, I cracked the first bottle. It was three fingers shy of rock bottom by eight. In the interim, Tinsel managed to smash his brand-new electric heater . . . Now the whole level was colder than ever. Sheets of ice encased each window. Only a gas stove, burning from all four ranges, emitted a field of lukewarm.

The room was a devastated wreck, as always. No one could generate a mess like Greetz. Piles of laundry across the floor. Broken bottles, overturned ashtrays. Teacups full of billowing mold, a plate of hardened garbanzo beans . . . And right in the middle, crowning the heap—aside from his bullhorn, front and center—a mound of text on robbing banks. "Preliminary groundwork," Tinsel called it: *"Knowledge is power—and power, the key!"*—though, once again, he'd expended more effort *stealing* material than he had reviewing it. If recent endeavors boded consistently, this one would land him in prison to stay.

"Well," he croaked from behind his accordion. "The Half-breed's looking reflective this evening. What gives in there?"

"Nothing." I shrugged. "Just picturing you in a four-by-seven."

"Oh, come *on*." He laughed. "We both know better. What's *really* amiss in that sozzled noggin? The Cong at Tet with the Bushmen again?"

"Or the Puritan lost in East St. Louis . . ."

"I wish I *was* a Puritan!" he said.

"Yeah. Burned at the stake in a week."

"Bah!" Scoffing, he threw back his shoulders. "Try telling *me* to get up on that stake . . . Shit. I wish I *was* a Puritan! Hoo-wee, I would *fuck* someone up!" He stood, veering, and tripped to the stove. "Bring my *own* fire down from the mountain!" Lighting a Merit on one of the ranges. Then, miming a swing of the pipe: "Just like with Ben— give 'em a taste of the Great White Oak!"

"You mean the Great White *Joke*."

"Whoa! *Dag!* A bit moody tonight?"

"Nah—" I looked at the bottle. "I'm fine."

"Hm." He considered. "I'm not so sure. Could be a ruse. Perhaps he frets the waning of our elixir?" He nudged the Scotch. "Is that it, Chuck? 'Whole world's a bottle and life, a dram / bottle goes empty, ain't worth a damn'?" Snapping forward, he raised his accordion. "Say, that calls for Ireland! Dig—"

On which he yodeled some raucous lament on the still going dry in the green hills of Doolin—although, in the process, he altered the lyrics to feature me as the woebegone subject. "Brian McDougal" became "Charlie McSpookel," and "Nurse a broken heart," "Born a breed apart" . . . crooning ungodly. Stomping the floor. Blasting his keyboard in throttled honks . . . It sounded like a chicken hawk cawing at a roadkill. I called for an end to it. Which only brought more.

Finally, I got up and left the room. A person can take only so much . . .

At length, the yodeling tapered off, but in its place came Wolfman Jack: "All right then, cats and dolls—there we had a bit of the old 'Genealogical Jumbalaya Blues' brought to you in honor of our spook in the bush: Mr. Hanoi Jackson, the Hereditary Carrefour . . ."

Reappearing, I sat on a milk crate. "You know," I said, "I've told you before—that Lenny Bruce shtick doesn't fly anymore. You do that in public, and people start looking to *me* to drag you out back, understand?"

"Hey, I don't need your charity, Jack."

"It has nothing to do with charity, Fuck-O. I'm just sick of bailing you out of jams. I'm not your bodyguard. *Or* your lawyer."

"Yeah, but you *are* the Half-breed." He winked, sneering, all *shucks* and *golly gee.* "I mean, it's not like I'm outright *lying* . . ."

*

I stared. He grinned.

I'd hit the wrong planet.

"All right, forget it!" I threw up my hands. "Like talking to a wall."

"Hey, I'm listening! *You're* the one not heeding the word. I told you about bringin' my fire from the mountain."

"Yeah, you told me." I waved him off. "Where's the bottle?"

He looked up. "What?"

"The bottle. Our Scotch. Where'd you put it?"

"Oh." He relaxed. "I meant to say—the bottle's gone empty."

"You finished it?"

"Yeah. There weren't much."

"Okay." I nodded. "So, where's the other?"

He drew a blank.

"The other bottle?" I coaxed him along.

"What other bottle?"

"The bottle we bought."

"*I* didn't buy—"

"The bottle *we* bought."

"Fine. I don't have it."

"Yes, you do." I glanced around. "I gave it to you. In the taxi. Earlier."

"Not I, Charles." Holding blank. "I thought *you* had the booze under wraps."

"You thought *I* . . . ?" A hot flash gripped me. "Listen: I gave you that bottle myself."

"No, you didn't."

"Yes, I *did*, you worthless prick! What did you do with it?" Storming circles. "What did you do with my Macallan's, Tinsel?"

"Cool down, Tiger."

I whirled, lashing. "*Never* call me Tiger!"

"Whoops." He giggled. "Sorry. 'Scuse . . . But seriously, man—cool your jets. No need for hysterics . . . After all, it's a quarter past eight. We've had our fill for the night, don't you think? I was considering turning in now." He feigned a stretch of exhaustion. "You know—get an early start. Up with the sun . . ."

"Don't give me that bullshit!"

"Sorry, Charlie."

"No 'sorry', either. Just fork up some money to go buy more."

He slapped his pockets. "I don't have money."

"What?"

"Yeah, it's back in the envelope."

"*What?*"

"The envelope, back in your bag—at the Desmon."

I wobbled. "The *Desmon*?"

He chewed on a cuticle. "Seemed like a good idea at the time. I thought we'd have breakfast at yours in the morning. Easier with cash already in the neighborhood."

The hot flash magnified. "What are you saying?"

He sneered. "Well, *you* left *your* money there."

I backed off, trying to get this straight, doing my best not to fall off the floor . . .

❄

First, he'd lost a bottle of top-shelf Scotch but couldn't remember where. Then, after netting a stack of pay, he'd left it clear across the tundra. And now, with nary a drop in the house, he'd drained our remaining fix on the sly. All of this done behind my back . . .

"What is *wrong* with you, Greetz?" I said.

"Hot damn!" He grabbed his bullhorn. "Thirsty little Half-breed!" Laughing, he blasted: **"HO CHI JONES ON THE WAGON BUT GOOD! HOP TO, CHARLIE!** *DIDI MAO!"*

I stood there, spinning in disbelief . . .

Squelching the last of *any*one's bottle, much less *mine*, with our present bearings (the liquor store closed, no cash on hand and the nearest deli a mile through the cold) was flat-out indecent by any standard. He knew what it meant to be left bone-dry. And he knew damn well that the change in my coat wouldn't cover a six-pack of *anything* bearable. It would have to be another Yellow Bull night, and that with no trolley fare left for the morning . . .

"Tinsel, you son of a bitch!" I blew.

"Wwhhooaahh!" He kicked his feet overhead. "Incoming!" Up with the bullhorn again: "What to do now? Put his **CHITLINS IN THE WOK, OR HIS HAWG JOWLS IN THE BUNJI PIT?"**

"*What* has gotten into you?"

He busted a gut . . . Whooping. Jeering. *Pleading* for the boot . . . I began to realize something was wrong here. Tactless the Anarchist may have been, but he wouldn't

(knowingly) run the risk of invoking the wrath, being tossed
out the window . . . No, there must be something else. He
was holding out on me. *Had* to be. *Surely* . . .

"All right, all right—" He gave in, sighing. "Your problem, Chuck, is that you jump to conclusions." He dropped
the horn and grabbed a bag from under the dresser. "I was
gonna keep going, but you're starting to froth. That being the
case . . ." He pulled out the bottle.

"*Give* me that!" I snatched it away.

Straight to the liver in four long gulps . . .

Tinsel, beaming, the moment I surfaced: "For a junior
welter, you *do* knock it back."

I wiped my chin and mouth, frowning. "Don't *ever* do
that again."

"Agreed. Sorry to push it, but I couldn't resist—you
looked too much like the Emperor Jones."

Shaking my head, I felt cold and alone.

There had to be somebody, *some*thing, out there . . .

He trundled over to wrap me in one of those sickly
endless blood-brother hippie hugs. "You're the greatest,
Charlie," he said. "I don't care what anyone says."

❊   ❊   ❊

At some point, we took to bashing plates and kicking up hell
with Tinsel's accordion. I was a slobbering wreck on my
crate, Greetz, an all-out conditional travesty—both of us

crowing dirge after ditty, hurling textbooks, pounding the wall. From two floors down, it must've sounded like a gaggle of maimed waterfowl fleeing the korn wolf.

Once the second bottle was finished, he carelessly pitched it over his shoulder. It smashed through a window, exploded outside. The wind howled in like death on a dock raft. All but one of the stove flames snuffed. I doubled over, laughing uncontrollably.

"You feel that, Chuck?" He held out his hand. "Hectic night for the meat-wagon crew."

He pulled out a hammer, nailed a blanket to the window. His pounding rocked the house. Plaster rained down. Smashing a footstool, he nailed that, too. Along with a desktop. Then a folding chair. I followed along, wrapped in a bedsheet, gobbing on the floor, berating his repair work . . .

That was the condition Zelda found us in.

"Tinsel!" The door flew open. "*Tinsel!*"

"What?" He spun, jumping out of his skin. "Whatsamatter? *Jesus . . .*"

"What's the *matter*?" She loomed. "You're raising the dead, and you ask what's *wrong*? . . . Look at this mess! What's happening here? . . . You didn't break the window. *Did you?*"

"No!" He threw up his hands. "It was one of those possums again. Damn thing . . . Slipped off the wire and *SMACK*. We were just sitting here. Right, Charlie?"

"Don't look at me . . ."

"You *idiots*!" she yelled. "It's freezing out there! . . . You promised you wouldn't be doing this . . . And . . . *eeyyuugghh* . . ." Retching, she backed away. "What died in here? It smells like Kong!" Regrouping, she blasted: "Look at you two! I asked you, Tinsel—I outright *implored* you! For just this once. To stay away . . ."

"Zelda, wait!" I cut in, confused. "What are you saying? I don't understand."

"What am I saying?" She drew back, infuriated. "What am I *saying*?" She hollered it now. "Ask *him*! He knows! I've told him for weeks!"

"*Weeks*?" said Tinsel. "Told me *what*?"

"I told you last Sunday, and I've reminded you Every. Single. Day. Since . . . that on Monday evening—THAT'S TONIGHT—at nine o'clock—THAT'S IN TEN MINUTES—I have an *extremely* important appointment with a photographic investor from Manhattan—AS IN *CIVILIZATION!* . . . I've put *six* months into this project. I'm not about to let you . . . *scumbags* . . . ruin it."

The Anarchist smirked. "So that's why you're so decked out," he mumbled.

"*What did you say?*"

"I said *that's* why you look like a French whore. The photographer. I forgot."

She froze, paralyzed. Tinsel went over and slipped her a kiss. She tore away, backed into the hall: "GET THE FUCK OUT OF HERE! BOTH OF YOU! NOW!"

Off her rocker. Bedlam in calico. Out of the game . . .

❋

It was time to leave.

Greetz shut the door, left her howling beyond. "I guess we could go to Maxine's," he suggested.

"All right," I agreed, grabbing my hat. "So long as we get out of *here* alive."

We pulled on our coats and killed the stove.

"You shouldn't have kissed her," I said.

"Yeah."

❀   ❀   ❀

On our way down the stairs, I swatted the back of his head. He spun, took a swing. Missed. His legs gave out. He rolled down the staircase. I hurdled him, made for the first flight, tripping . . . Behind me, I heard him get to his feet. Closing fast, right on my heels. He tackled me, hard. We fell to the landing. Wiped out a table. Plates on the floor . . . Zelda careened from the kitchen, irate . . . We got up, opened the door, stumbling. Fell through the screen. Hit the porch . . . I grabbed his jacket. He pulled my hair . . . We pitched down the staircase, end over end . . . Hitting the street, regained our footing . . . I grabbed a bottle, let fly. Missed . . . He picked up a can, returning fire. It clipped me . . . I stumbled—into a car . . . Jumped on its hood. Tinsel followed . . . I leapt up top. *Bang*—to the trunk. *Thud*—to the next. All down the block.—*Bang, thud. Bang, thud.* In rapid succession, hooting like apes . . . *Bang, thud. Bang, thud. Bang, thud. BOOM.*

❀

I wasn't conscious of making the jump. The oncoming Ford never caught my attention. I only registered falling just as my skull hit the windshield. And thereafter: *change* . . .

I dropped to the pavement, flat on my back. Tires ground to a halt beside me. A door flew open. Shouts: "*Motherfucker!*" Boots touching down. Coming around . . . Then: SLAM, to the jaw . . . Back to the pavement. Peering up. And SLAM, again . . .

Blood in my mouth. Hot, salty—spilling in patches, across the asphalt . . .

Rolling over, I got to my feet and staggered away, hands in the air. Once at the curb, I turned for a look: two brothers in skullcaps bathed in the headlights—one with a pile jack cocked to strike, the other built like a Jersey shithouse—both advancing with cold, wild violence diffusing every gesture . . .

The first took a swing. I dodged in time, then continued withdrawing, real diplomatic . . . Fighting it out was never an option. Not this one. No *way in hell* . . . Being stewed, outnumbered, bleeding and at *fault,* I didn't stand a chance. Besides, they were *huge* . . . Blind retreat was my only alternative. No shame in that. Screw heroics.

I kept backing off, palms outturned, acknowledging blame on every count. Then, from the shadows, Tinsel appeared—baying and stomping and waving his arms. The Skullcaps turned. "Cowards!" he yelled. They started after him. I was left standing . . .

❊

A vacant patch of concrete surrounded me. The Ford sat empty, its engine running. Giant speakers boomed from within: "Welcome to the *Terrordome*."

Here we go again.

Down the street, all hell let loose — a blitz of combustible, senseless mayhem: the Skullcaps lunging steadily forward, swiping their jack while bellowing wildly, Tinsel retreating in backward leaps, ducking and shuffling, just out of reach — their voices combined in garbled dissonance echoing west down Baltimore Ave., with Greetz's blue-faced cri de coeur to *stay the fuck back!* overriding all . . .

Bad, rampant criminal havoc. And all my fault. I had to do *something*.

I ran down the block, came up from behind. Got to Tinsel, told him to cool it. He didn't listen, just kept on screaming. I'd never seen him so utterly crazed . . . I turned to the Skullcaps, begged them to stop. They drove us through a line of parked cars . . . Porch lights flashed. A dog was barking. Shouts let out from open windows.

Possible tombstone inscription #1: CHARLES EVANS, URBAN STATISTIC.

There's really no telling how long it lasted. Combat rolls to a beat of its own. By the time they split, it seemed ages had passed. But given the muddle, it could have been seconds.

I was prepared to bask in the calm as a sudden reprieve from the firing squad. But not so Tinsel. Still on a rampage. Taking my head in both hands, he hollered: "LOOK WHAT THEY DID TO YOUR FACE, CHARLIE!"

I tried to assure him it couldn't touch me, these antics were pointless.

To no avail.

"Pansy *bastards*!" he yelled up the street. And soon they were back, with *bats* this time. The whole thing resumed, only worse than before—down the block, all over again: Tinsel the madman, Charlie the gimp, Skullcaps swinging their cracker sticks wide—pure, adrenalized rage and confusion . . .

#2: KILLED BY STUPIDITY.

After a while, I think Tinsel started to give them the creeps. Fear of contagion.

Once they turned to leave a second time, I *ordered* him not to speak . . .

Still no good. Too keyed up, storming the walk in reckless abandon. "LOOK WHAT THEY DID TO YOUR FACE!" he repeated.

"Forget it!" I hissed. "It's nothing. *Be quiet!*"

But that didn't fly. And neither would threats. In this state, reason was lost on Greetz.

He spun and kicked a bakery window. Slabs of glass rained down on the pavement. Inside the store, an alarm went off. Then streetlights, neighbors, ten thousand dogs . . .

*

#3: EVANS DREAMED OF QUIET NIGHTS IN DALE, INDIANA.

Veering, blood-soaked from collar to crotch, I gurgled, "*Uhlk*," out on my feet. Tinsel looked over as though to concur, bewildered at last. Back from beyond . . .

"Maybe we ought to get going," he said.

I spluttered accord.

We ran down an alley.

*   *   *

I know our reentry was hell for Zelda—I take no pride in recounting as much. However, at least Zelda *knew* us. The rumored "investor" wasn't so fortunate.

She (it turned out) had been in the house for a whopping total of ninety seconds—an already frazzled Zelda had greeted her, taken her coat and adjourned to the den when Greetz and I appeared at the back, crocked, mangled and raving, insane . . .

I picture it now, step by step: a distant rumble approaching the courtyard—cursing and yelling, trash cans flying, scrap lumber hitting the patio in stacks—then Tinsel busting in on a road rage, dishpans hitting the floor behind him, Zelda losing her cool in a flash: "No! Jesus! No! No!"—the wall-mounted radio leading from *All Things Considered* to Glenn Gould's Bach in C minor, and one joggled and lacerated half-breed tripping to the sink to vomit his guts out . . .

To hell with poor taste: *nuke* the welcome wagon.

*

I didn't spot her right away. I couldn't turn without spraying the counter. Introductions were out of the question. Besides, I hadn't examined myself.

Priority one: damage assessment.

For all I could tell, my jaw was intact. No teeth were missing. Both eyes were in place . . . All the rest was up in the air. The pain hadn't hit. But the blood had. *Gobs* of it: swirling the drain with the Scotch and pizza and gastric bile from the pit of my gut. I heaved uncontrollably, head to the faucet—nose chucking marinara, Bach in C minor . . .

Tinsel and Zelda at war in the hall—her voice a bomb blast between clenched teeth, Greetz less reserved, kicking the wall—both in a high-strung Mexican standoff till, finally, Zelda broke down completely, wailing and crying and blasting us both as heartless, disgraceful alcoholic bastards . . .

Somewhere in there my legs gave out. I pitched over backward. My head hit the wall. A water jug fell on top of me, crashing. I wound up sprawled in the corner, soaked.

I must have blacked out for a minute or two—the change to B major eluded my ear. Once it registered, someone was touching me: hands on my forehead, soothing, delicate . . . Dimly, I wondered: *Postmortem reverie? . . . Dead on the floor with my head busted open? . . .* But then I heard Tinsel and realized no, I hadn't left the kitchen. I was still in the corner. Someone was touching me. Someone incredible . . .

I opened my eyes.

And there she was . . .

Slowly, her facial components merged, one at a time,
to a faultless composite, starting with the jaw: a delicate
ridge panning back and away with impeccable symmetry
. . . hair, full-bodied, black, luxuriant, framing a wide,
unfurrowed brow . . . skin, a warm tone of alabaster,
smooth as marble with no trace of blemish, gently defin-
ing a flow of contours: high-set cheekbones, supple lips,
a rounded nose and chin dipping, curving gracefully down
to her neck . . . and back to the eyes—greenish orbs, endless, piercing, attentive, alert—the gaze, searching, though
deeply rooted, disarming yet somehow safety incarnate.
All-consuming. Omnipresent. Oases of calm in a sea of
disorder . . .

"Are you all right?" came a voice from afar.

All I could do was gawk in reply.
    The soundtrack cut.
    Denial ensued . . .
    I must've been dreaming, must've been *dead* . . .
    What else would account for a vision this fair?
    Scotch?
    Impossible.
    Concussion?
    Perhaps.
    Death?
    Unlikely . . .
    But *how*, then?

*

HOW?

No matter / regardless / whatever the case:

If this be the wine of madness, keep going . . .

Beat me with rake handles.
    Drown me in scrapbooks.
    Force-feed me chart readings.
    Show me that mercy . . .
    Strap me in hawk wire, throw me a bone, just
    whatever you do, please —
    don't go away . . .

A pounding erupted. Tinsel ran in. "Cops, Charlie! On your feet!"

Not now, Greetz, I'm dying down here . . .

"Charlie! Move it! *Cops* on the stoop!"
The pounding resumed. Zelda again, screaming of cruisers and killing us both . . .
I groped to my feet. Tinsel took over, shoving me, fucker . . .
Flat on my face.

    Gone.

"Come ON!"

Forever . . .

❀

"Charlie!"

*Rugburn. Pounding. "OPEN UP!" *Glenn Goulð.**

"Damn it, Breed! You won't like the catacombs. *Rape,* man—*RAPE!*"

I got up, determined . . .
　　The stairs, a blur.
　　A hatch came open. Tinsel went through . . .
　　I followed along, onto a blacktop. Out of the death car. Into the night . . .

LOUISE

The formula stands: thaw one derelict, douse with toxins, marinate in rotgut and beat to a pulp, then cool in a black, dreamless void and set to rise on the other half's turf . . .

Voilà: Nancy Reagan's Revenge. Serves none.

It might have been an ICU on the mother ship. God knows, it was posh enough. All around me in lavish abundance: candelabras, mahogany chairs, brocade curtains, a whitewashed ceiling . . . It wasn't the Desmon, that's for certain — no panic, alarms or drilling outside . . . In place of my beer-stained Navajo blanket, I was smothered in goose down, clean, soft sheets. The bed was enormous, the silence unreal . . . I was somewhere new, warm and unturbulent. Alone. With another bed to one side. Slept in. No idea by whom.

❊

Simply lifting my head was the killer: an all-points alert to worldly agony . . . Two pounds of silage in both ailing lungs. A hatchet cleaving my forehead in two. Esophagus lurching Tobasco and egg whites, red-hot alloy lodged in the gut . . .

I curled up, helplessly gripping my skull, locked in a cross-eyed fetal knot.

These are the moments the surgeon general warns you about . . .

I noticed the bandage. Gauze at my brow, clipped into place . . . Someone had tended me, taken my shirt. My skin smelled of soap. I was fitted in night pants, silk, paisley . . . What it all meant, I had no idea. How I'd gotten there, when, nothing . . .

I looked around.

Where the hell *was* I?

It almost looked like an upscale hotel room . . .

Slowly, I rose to a sitting position. The first wave of nausea hit like a pork bomb. I sallowed over, coiled to hurl. But the chamber was empty. No ammunition.

Somehow I managed to slide my legs across the mattress and over its edge. I straightened up. My feet hit the floor. Gripping the bed rail, I caught my breath.

This part was critical; as they say — *walking relies on not falling down.*

I started forward, one league at a time. Clear to the mirror. In for a look . . .

My lip was torn, swollen and oozing. A lavender shiner from jaw to temple. Gravel-torn bruises, goose eggs, abrasions . . .

I looked like a rotting glob of liver.

Turning away, I limped to the window and, squinting, partially drew the blinds . . . Snow lined rooftops for miles on end. Office buildings. Cathedral spires. Two hundred yards over Central Main, overlooking the academy . . . It *was* a hotel.

Below, the entire block had been sealed, traffic re-routed to either side. From curb to curb, a line of trailers jammed the street, their lift gates open. Twenty or thirty freezing technicians darted about, erecting equipment. Maybe Savalitch had finally gone loco: Verdi at rush hour and thirty below.

Then I heard Tinsel's voice through the wall. Speaking tongues. What was he saying?

I walked to a door at the end of the room. It creased to an optical liquidation. I shielded my eyes, blinded: Cave Breed—wandering aimless, into the void . . .

"Hold on, Daddy!" came Tinsel's voice.

The room materialized, bit by bit . . . Bureaus. Recliners. Wall-to-wall carpeting . . . Lamp shades. Television. Polished oak tables . . . A platter cart—teapots, cutlery, bread . . . And last, in between, the two of them, staring –

Greetz in satin, stroking his bullhorn, Madame Serenity, looking me over—both in mute anticipation, expectant, wide-eyed, awaiting the verdict . . .

"What happened?" I mumbled.

They broke down laughing.

Tinsel swept some cash from the table. "I *told* you he wouldn't remember! Hoo!" He turned to me, flashing a five-dollar bill. "You just bought us lunch!" He laughed, turning back. "I *told* you he wouldn't remember! I *knew* it!"

Wouldn't remember *what*, I wondered . . .

Causing a scene in the lobby downstairs? Wiping out coat racks? Soiling the lift? . . . Or was it something else? Something much worse. Something said while she tended my wounds? Some heinously incriminating, asinine remark . . . Or plural: *remarks* . . . Things concerning *her* . . .

No, I didn't remember that. No, I was *glad* I didn't remember that.

I don't dig my naked ape on display.

"What's happening outside?" I changed the subject. "Some kind of project down in the street . . ."

"Ah, that—" said Tinsel, sitting up. "You may find this hard to believe, Charlie, but *that* is Delvin Corollo's troop. They're shooting a film. *The Season of Innocence.*"

"Corollo?" I spluttered. "*That* is Corollo?"

"Yes." He rose and hobbled over. "They're sealing the block for a 'winter scene' . . . Horse and buggies. Top hats.

Something . . . The bellhop said a 'Victorian epic.' Two million dollars of preparation for a nine-second shot. It's enough to make you sick."

"When are they shooting?"

"Tonight. *Late.* They want 'minimal interference' from the public."

"*Minimal interference?*"

"Yeah, ain't that awful? Tie up center city for days, then ward off the public as an *inconvenience.*"

I shook my head. "So where's your paint gun?"

"Back at the house."

"Oh." The "house" took a moment to register. Then, cringing: "Oh, yeah. The *house* . . ."

Tinsel, grimly: "That's right, Chaz—with everything else. Except for *this.*" He held up the bullhorn. "She would've destroyed it."

"*Destroyed* it?" I buried my face. "We're lucky if Zelda doesn't *kill* us."

"Don't worry about that," a voice interrupted. "I'll handle Ms. Deeds this afternoon."

Losing my bearings, I looked around. And that's all the longer it took to hit me . . . There on the love seat. Wrapped in satin. Knees in hand, basking, radiant . . . Who *was* this woman? —*Zelda had said*—and why was she staring at me that way? —"*an investor from Manhattan*"—exuding self-certainty—"*as in CIVILIZATION!*"—gazing me down. *But not Yankee-born, surely.* With a look of recognition. *The skin's a dead giveaway.* Intimate, assuming . . . *Euro, no doubt.* What was she doing here? *Danish? Italian?* On business in Philth Town? *The Baltimore projects?* It didn't seem possible . . . *Lost or insane.* An island, regardless. *Filthy rich, too.* And sweet-Jesus beautiful . . .

I couldn't even look at her.

Forgetting to ask about Zelda, I sat.

Tinsel smirking across the table. "Good one last night," he said. "No?"

I didn't respond. I'd just blown in on the tails of a death wind . . .

"I *said,*" he repeated, "that was *good* last night, don't you think?"

"Right!" Attempting to ward him off.

He drew back, confused. "What's this?" he asked, looking to *her* as though she'd know. "What's wrong with Charlie? Finest night he's had in weeks, and all he can say is *right*? . . . I don't get it."

"Give me a minute!" I snapped. "Please. I just woke up."

We sat in silence.

There were cigarettes. There was coffee. And there was bacon, *Jesus* . . .

I picked up a paper, trying to look occupied. Leafing through it, came to a blurb: some town in Kentucky recalling a trash strike. REDNECK INFERNO, the title read.

"There was a garbage strike in Kentucky," I announced.

"Oh, yeah?" Grinning, Tinsel looked up. "You ought to go to Kentucky sometime."

"Why's that?" I asked.

"They'd love you there . . ."

Moments later, I ran out of coffee. The investor claimed there was more in the bedroom. I went to find it, still not clear on why she hadn't thrown us out.

Standing by the mirror when she called my name. "Charlie!"

She knew it.

"Yes?" I replied.

"Will you grab my belt while you're in there, please?"

"Sure." *Mrs. Robinson, ho hum.* "Coming."

I looked around. Her belt, her belt . . . It wasn't on the dresser. It wasn't on the floor. It *definitely* wasn't in my bed . . . I drew aside the blankets on the second mattress . . . There it was. Along the edge . . . But there was something else. Something with it . . . A sock. A filthy, horrible sock. *Tinsel's* sock . . . Between the sheets. With *her* lingerie. In the same bed . . .

"Did you find it?" she called.

"Yeah, one minute."

I wheeled back in and presented the belt. She took it, grinning. "Thank you. Now, is that coffee still warm?" She touched the pot. "No, it's not. I'll order more."

"No!" I yelled. "Sorry, but . . ." *Filthy, horrible.* "Drink coffee cold — like a wolf!"

"Like a what?" she asked.

"Like a *wolf,* I think he said," Tinsel laughed.

She frowned. "I didn't know wolves drank coffee."

"Sure they do!" *Why?* "Heard it on a billboard!"

Greetz kept laughing.

"Come on," she insisted. "I'll order more . . ."

"No!" I blurted. "Thanks, but really—it's better this way!"

And just to prove it, I grabbed the pot and started guzzling. Straight down a lung . . . Choking, snot-thrown, hosing the table. "'scuse, I . . ." *Jackass.* "Can't get . . ." *Shoot me.*

"Are you all right?" she asked.

"Great!" *for an invalid.* "The coffee's great, too! Thanks!" She didn't look convinced.

"Really!" I spluttered, wiping my face. "It was just this . . ." *Moron.* "You know, this—" *Goddamn.* ". . . handle got lockjaw, strapped into . . ." *STOP* it! " . . . over though, basically—back to your normal."

Drop the hammer NOW, please . . .

She started forward, concerned. I was gripped with a sudden impulse to get up and run.

"Let's see." She cradled my head in her hands and tipped it back, into the light.

Greetz snickering, hideous bastard.

"I think these cuts are superficial," she muttered to no one in particular. "But you *may* have a concussion. Are you feeling dizzy?"

"No!"

"Hm . . ." The exam continued. "Maybe I *should* call a doctor. Yes?"

"NO! NO!" On the brink of screaming. "Thanks, but . . . No. Doctors. *Please*."

She straightened up, seeming vaguely dissatisfied. "Well, all right then. If you say so. I *guess* . . . But *do* speak up if you start feeling sick. We can make a call." She backed away. "Now. If the two of you will excuse me, I have to take care of some things downstairs." She stepped into slippers and made for the door. "If you need more coffee, just dial reception. And Charlie—there's another shirt in the closet. Your last one scared the maid to death."

Once she was gone, a pigeon appeared at the window, glaring: *Kick his ass, Chuck!* . . .

In the right state of being, I might've complied. But this was *hardly* the right state of being. I was enfeebled, and Greetz, oblivious . . . Combat would only disgrace the species.

The pigeon retreated as dignity spurned, leaving the Anarchist scot-free, babbling.

"So." He leered with a shit-eating grin, his arms spread wide, chewing a Merit. "What do you think? Did you know hotels went up to five stars? *Look* at this place!"

I started right in. "What happened last night?"

He shook his head. "You really don't remember?"

"No, I don't."

"That's the *fourth* time this month."

"I know. Tell me."

"All right, let's see . . ." Rolling his eyes, he dragged on the butt, then broke it down: "The cops barged in while we were on the roof . . . Tore the house to pieces, put Zelda through the ringer, gave Frogger the shakedown—papers, Visa, passport, everything . . ."

I cut in. "Where's she from?"

"*Her?*"

"Yeah."

He blinked. "Are you kidding?"

"No."

"*France,* fool. Can't you hear it?"

"No."

"All right, her English *is* good. I'll grant you that," he conceded, nodding. "But she's no Canuck, if that's what you mean. No, that's *real* French. She's from the *banlieue.*"

"The *what?*"

"Paris, monoglot! What did you think I said—the *bayou?*"

"But what about Manhattan?"

"Listen, your guess is as good as mine. I have no idea." He cleared his throat. "Anyway . . . the cops threw her out on the street. She got in her car, made the first turn. And that's where we came into the picture."

"I thought you said we were up on the roof?"

"We were—*before* the alley. *After* the fire escape. Doesn't ring a bell?"

"No," I admitted.

"*You* collapsed in a pile of trash. *I* ran into the road . . ?"

Something caught: "I *do* remember you up on a hood."

"Yeah, well . . ." He soured over. "My mark was off, what do you expect? The headlights were blinding, and *you* were no help . . ."

"All right, never mind that. What happened next?"

"Oh, *man!*" He slapped a palm to his forehead. "You should have seen their *faces*, Charlie . . . The doorman, especially—almost had a coronary. Bellhops, too . . . You were a *mess.*"

"No, not that. I mean *after* that."

"Well . . ." He drifted beyond his punch line into a dead zone. "I don't know. We doctored you up and put you to bed. That's pretty much it."

"*And?*"

"And what?"

"And what happened then?"

"What are you talking about?"

"I mean what *happened*—you know exactly!"

He shifted, hedging. "What's wrong with you?"

"Did you sleep with her?"

No, say no, please, no . . .

"Look," he tried to let it pass, "it was a long night."

I grabbed his arm. "DID YOU *SLEEP* WITH HER?"

"Whoa!" Tearing away. "Hands off, Jack! Don't push your luck."

"All right, all right—sorry. Just tell me. I only want to know . . . Did you *sleep* with her?"

No . . .

He crushed his smoke in the tray, then leaned back, shrugging. "Why? Wouldn't you?"

❋

Damn it.

❋   ❋   ❋

The elevator suffered: twenty-one floors of NO EXIT with a
prune in a blue chinchilla . . . warding off visions of jamming
the elevator, punching through the ceiling hatch, scaling its
cable . . . I split that car like a plague-infected water hole,
weaving through the lobby, straight for an exit . . . Along the
way, corporate types flew by—hair care, dry cleaning, paper-
work, order . . . I kept on moving—through a mob of bag-
hands, underneath a chandelier, around a marble fountain . . .
I was almost clear when she called my name. "Charlie!"

I froze—*nailed* in my tracks.

She was moving toward me, closing fast. Again I felt
that impulse to run.

She stepped up. "What do you think you're doing?"

"I'm late for work," I said. "Gotta go."

"What?" She paused. "You mean you're not staying?"

"Hello?"

"I said: you're not staying with me?"

"You're serious."

"Of *course* I'm serious, silly. We haven't even been in-
troduced yet. I'm Louise Gascoygne." She held out her hand.
I gave it a pump, then tore away.

"Evans. Charlie . . . Listen, thanks. For everything.
Really. And sorry about last night."

"Oh?" She smiled. "That's not what your friend says."

"Yeah, well. My friend says a lot."

"I'm sure he does," she said. "But that's no excuse for you stealing away."

"Right." I clutched. "But, you know, I'm just a—" *Coward.* "On element—"*Over my—* "*edge,* I mean—*out* of mine. Not used to this kind of . . ."

"What—*hotel?*"

"Yeah." *Right, blame it on the building.* "Well, not exactly . . . I mean, I *live* in a . . . "—shitty—"hotel myself. But not like . . . How to say?" *Xanadu.* "Not like . . ."

"*This.*" She nodded, looking around. "I know. I feel the same way. But you must understand, our rooms are booked in advance. I can find somewhere else if you want me to."

"*What?*"

"I said: we can go somewhere else if it's *too* much here."

"Why the *ffff* . . ." *Watch it.* "'Scuse." *&*&¢%$#@#$* (*Steady*): "*Why* would you do that?"

"Because—" Her expression slowly drifted from requiescence to mortal dread. "You're staying here, aren't you? . . . You're not going to leave me alone with *him?*"

Finally, a break.

She didn't want to be alone with the Anarchist. Ha! Maybe she *wasn't* insane . . .

Ready to throw in the towel, I asked her: "Do you have any idea what you're doing?"

"Yes." She held out a pen and paper. "Please. Give me your address at work."

I scribbled the coordinates, still at a loss.

"When do you finish?" she asked.
"Six. I'm already late. I have to go—"
"Wait!" She caught my wrist.

ε3¢%$#@#$%¢ε3@#%¢%$#@*ε3¢%$#@*ε3¢%$#@
*ε3¢ %$#@

"*Easy*, now," she said. "It's all right . . ."
Reaching out, she adjusted the bandage.
I almost threw my tubular cast.
"There. Better." She backed off, smiling. "Relax, will
you?"

She walked away.

THE GRIND

I got to the deli at 11:08 to find Hanz the Dutchman seething with impatience behind the till, where he'd been all morning.

"Em-ah, Charles!" he exploded on contact. "Howzt going? Nice of you to drop by!" He gave me a thoroughly revolted once-over, then resumed with streamlined vitriol: "Exciting evening, I take it. Hm-ah, yes, well—*pity*." He cleared his throat. "So, then—moving right along—" He presented an almost *comically* brutal list of duties, from till repair to septic maintenance, all of which had been growing in size and severity over the past three hours. By now it read more like the annual quota for a road gang than deli work.

Here went nothing . . .

Five minutes later I was down in the cellar sweeping piles of rat shit from every corner. The Dutchman had thrown me a dingy old broom and a pan with no handle. I wasn't getting anywhere . . . Nothing on the level was working worth a damn — lightbulbs, wall heaters, switch boxes, *me* . . . In vain, I clambered over mounds of furniture, pitching down the incline, gagging through hot sweats . . . I may as well have been back in the sewers, only now I was *cleaning up after* Ben. Rapid downward mobility, that: from holy terror to underpaid housemaid . . .

I wouldn't have lasted as either that morning.

Once the corners were swept and cleared — to add to matters, insult, injury — I was meant to load the elevator full of Old Mud and run it to the stockroom upstairs. In my condition, I didn't even want to *look* at beer, much less handle it.

I got three cases into the lift and was turning for a fourth when the door slid shut . . .

I'd forgotten to hold the car.

A motor rattled. I panicked, furiously jamming the call button. It didn't respond. The needle climbed to four. Then *stopped* . . .

It stayed there for a *long* time. I was trapped in the cellar, kicking myself for an idiot. Someone upstairs (probably that blue-haired dolt with the pit bull) was waking to a stack of swill from out of the sky, free of charge . . .

And, of course, the car came back empty. Bastards . . . Hanz would have a conniption when he found out. *Charles!* — And he *would* find out. *How is this POSSIBLE?* Then dock my pay. *Fifty dollars!* One more time. *Tell it goodbye!*

＊

I collapsed on the floor.

It seems the Grim Reaper had standards that day . . .

After a while, a large black cockroach crawled into view on a pipe overhead. Outside of the Desmon, I'd never seen bigger—probably had a wingspan of six to eight inches. I thought about catching him to plant in the till for the queens on the night shift. *There* was a thought: none of Hanz's graveyard club boys would have been caught in this hole for a second. They were clean, they were gay, and they did *not* go down in the cellar, thank you very much. All grunt labor was relegated my way, left for the token straight boy on the day shift. Which *usually* wasn't a problem. I relished the solitude, rat shit and all . . .

However, on mornings like this, it was heinous—worse than the Willard Rounds, by far—enough to warrant storming upstairs, grabbing the pasty bitch by his collar and tossing him down the shaft with orders to clear the whole level for white-glove treatment . . . I told myself no: I was too levelheaded, far too *rational,* for such drastic measures . . . But that was a crock. Levelheaded. Shit. Try *cowardly,* maybe. Or just plain *incapable* . . .

Anyway, cellar duty wasn't the problem. Rat shit hadn't reduced me to this. And neither had a hangover (albeit crippling), *or* a host of potential fractures . . . It was that Gascoygne woman back at the hotel, damn it. Something about that investor had floored me. And here, on the uptake, my system was reeling—racked by tides of bliss and anxiety

. . . In part, I ached as a blubbering ham: a grade-A sap case pining for eternity . . . But more so, I felt entirely *exposed* . . . Found out. Stark naked. Transparent. *Seen* . . . And not without reason. After all, it was true: I'd spewed my visceral load on the table and, in the end, been met with no more than a casual, fleeting suggestion to *relax* . . .

How the *fuck* was I meant to relax?

How to "relax" when her mere *appearance* had cost me a wholesale cut in intelligence?

How to "relax" when her every gesture had robbed my basic capacity for speech?

How to "relax" after blowing our intro with all the poise of a simpering cretin?

How to "relax"—to face the world, myself or *anyone,* now, in *this* state?—when all it might take to level me flat was a byte from "Total Eclipse of the Heart"?

That's when you know you've got it bad—when all the wrong sap ditties start making sense . . .

Aye, no doubt: I was screwed something terrible. Out of the running. Flat-out fucked. Contradictory urges tormented me—every impulse unleashing a counterpart. Longing to see this woman at six but praying to Christ she'd never show. Pining for hours on end by her side, while knowing another *minute* could finish me. Dying to crawl back and lounge in her suite when, in truth, I belonged right there, where I was: in the cellar. Alone. Out of harm's reach. A threat to no one and nothing but mine.

❄ ❄ ❄

The Dutchman rode herd all morning.

After the stockroom, he sent me to a second-level storage vault across the lot to haul three ninety-pound air conditioners down a long flight of stairs. (Air conditioners in the middle of February.) Busting my balls every step of the way. "The walls, the walls! Mind the *walls*!"

Next I was ordered to scour the toilet and sinks, which hadn't been cleaned in a month. Followed by a lengthy mop job of the entire heap-cluttered back room. Along with a trip to the post office on foot — clear over to Thirteenth and back in the brutal cold — with a fifteen-minute time limit, which I *still* overshot by half an hour . . . And continuing with plow duty: hand-chipping ice from the walk along the storefront, patch by painstaking patch, until the ravaged old pick handle busted in three.

"This lasted seventeen years before *you* got ahold of it!"

By the time the Dutchman's lover, her ever-so-scrutinizing highness Ramesh, appeared in skin-tight Calvin Kleins and a hot-pink ski coat, I was stripping down the slicer to meet Hanz's newfound "sanitary standards."

"Em-ah, you never know when the health board might drop by!" he announced.

Right. The health board.

This was the living *epitome* of a tax dodger who sent down-and-out types into the abyss to clear the shit at $4 an hour, and he was talking *regulations*?

❄

"These soup cans look awful!" Ramesh whined.

The Dutchman went over to see for himself. They mumbled back and forth for a moment, then: "Em-ah, Charles! Come here!"

I walked around the counter, into the aisle.

"NO!" Hanz yelled. "Bring the price gun! Use your brain!" He turned to Ramesh and shook his head, cutting me down till I reappeared. "Now. Price these cans! They look horribly. I don't know why you did it this way in the first place."

"I didn't price these cans."

"Of course you priced them! And they look disgusting! Price it! . . . No, not like that! . . . Peel off the old ticket first . . . Scrape it! Move it along . . . There! Now price it! . . . No! Not on the side, fool! On top! You see—on *TOP*! Why do you think it was wrong to begin with? . . . And . . . Wait . . . What is this? . . . There's no *tape* in this gun! . . . How can you price anything without tape? . . . Get the roll. Quickly! . . . GET THE ROLL!! . . . No! Not from there. The *left* drawer! *LEFT!* You know the difference? . . . There. Now. Load it . . . LOAD IT! . . . No, you're doing it wrong! . . . Give it to me! See: you take *this* little roll, and you place it on *this* little peg . . . and WOWZA! . . . See what happens when you use your brain? It's amazing . . . Now. Price it. Price it! . . . MY GOD, NO! What are you doing? Look at this . . . You've got the wrong price! . . . It says thirty-nine cents here—your price . . . These cans should be ONE thirty-nine. Do you hear me? ONE THIRTY-NINE! . . . You're off by a whole dollar! . . . What have I done to provoke such incompetence? . . . Change it! Hurry! . . . There. Now. Price it! . . . BAH, that's terrible! You tore the edges! Take it off! Do it again!

NOW! . . . Wait, what's happening here? . . . YOU LEFT THE *DELI* CASE OPEN? . . . CHARLES! For the love of God, what are you thinking? . . . MEAT SPOILS!"

"But you told me to come over here—"

"I DIDN'T TELL YOU TO DESTROY THREE HUNDRED DOLLARS' WORTH OF STOCK! What's the matter with you? Move it! Now!"

I walked to the deli and started shoveling blocks of cheese back into the case. Somewhere along the way, I dropped a chunk of alpine Swiss on the floor. The impact boomed like a tumbling oak. Hanz wheeled over in a tizzy. "What happened, what happened? You . . . *dropped* . . . ?"

I picked up the cheese, brought it around. A film of dirt coated one end.

"LOOK AT THIS! I can't *believe* such incredibility! What am I expected to—" He choked, infuriated. Then, exploding: "CUT OFF THE END! Don't waste anything! No, not with the knife! The slicer, the slicer!"

But the slicer was disassembled . . .

"What *is* this?" He turned.

"You told me to clean the equipment."

"That was *twenty* minutes ago! What have you been doing all this time?"

"I was—"

"NEVER MIND! NO EXCUSES! GET ME A KNIFE! MOVE! QUICKLY!"

I was fishing through the sink when Bob, the second cashier, who'd arrived at noon, appeared from an extended trip to the freshly shined toilet. He rounded the corner whistling an old show tune, then suddenly tripped and fell into Ramesh. Together, they rammed a product rack, throwing soap and toilet paper everywhere. The Dutchman shot from the deli area. "WHAT HAPPENED? WHAT NOW?"

"Who left these cans all over the floor?" Bob demanded, clutching one knee.

"It was Charles!" Ramesh cried.

Hanz whirled. "How is this possible? What in the EARTH has gotten into you? Clean up these cans! Clean them up! . . . Now, before you kill someone!"

"But what about the deli? You said—"

"Never mind! Clean up the cans!"

I walked into the aisle once more. The Dutchman stormed back to the deli. Bob remained with his shoulder to the rack. Ramesh loomed, on the brink of tears.

A customer came in.

"I'm not going to make it!" cried Bob.

"Em-ah, Charles!" Hanz yelled. "Tend to the sale. Quickly!"

"But the cans—"

"Never *mind* the cans!"

I walked to the front register. It was locked. "I need the key!"

Bob dug into his pocket and lobbed me the key. It glanced off the counter, hit the wall. I stooped to find it. But couldn't somehow . . . I checked the floor. Under the counter. Behind the bags . . . Nowhere. Gone.

The customer waited, tapping one foot. The Dutchman was cursing back in the corner. Bob and Ramesh, swooning in the aisle . . .

"I can't find the key!" I announced, cringing.

All three of them hobbled out of the aisle like bloodthirsty villagers.

"What did you say?"

"Bob threw me his—"

"NO EXCUSES! LORD GOD—GET AWAY FROM THAT REGISTER!"

"Clean up the aisle!" yelled Bob. "At least do *one* thing right."

"What's that kid's problem?" the customer asked.

"No one knows," Ramesh answered.

I went back to the aisle. Soup cans, soap and toilet paper everywhere. The deli case open, its window fogged and splotched with Windex—the slabs of meat inside, cockeyed. Dirt-smeared alpine Swiss on the counter. The slicer in pieces. The ice pick, broken. Ramesh, Bob and the Dutchman frantically tearing the front of the store to pieces . . .

Right about then, an English girl from around the corner came by for a beer. She passed the scene up front, dug into the case and walked to the deli register. I went over to ring her up.

"And may I have some crisps and a pack of fags as well?" she asked.

I stuffed the beer and chips in a bag while explaining how smokes were collected up front. Then, without pausing to think, I turned and yelled to Bob: "PACK OF FAGS!"

All three of them whirled in mid-harangue, as though to say "Ex-*CUSE* us?"

✻

At that point I lost my head completely. I couldn't
help it. Resistance was futile . . . Any attempt to explain
would have bombed, and, it goes without saying, apolo-
gies were out . . . All I could do was laugh uncontrollably.
And not healthy laughter, either — more like *sick, wounded
hysteria* . . .

*   *   *

Before long, the pain in Bob's knee grew so unbearable that
Hanz sent him home. Then, at two-thirty, the Dutchman
himself left for the distributor to load up on stock. Ramesh
vanished shortly thereafter, leaving me to hold down the
store alone. I plugged in the radio just in time for Act I of
Götterdämmerung, then set about tearing into the Pop-Tarts,
washing them down with a quart of eggnog and preparing
to milk that goddamned register for every other dollar that
came through the store.

After a while, Armless Rob swaggered in. "Hey,
Chuck! Alone in paradise?"

"Seems that way."

"I thought so. Mind if I grab a beer?"

I waved him on.

He walked to the case to eye the selection. "How's the
Belhaven?"

"Good for the season."

"Yeah? Okay if I grab a bottle?"

"Take six. They're below."

"*Yes!*" He kicked off a shoe and opened the door. "I
won't forget this, man." He dragged a pack from the lowest

shelf and carefully slid it down the aisle. I met him halfway, unfolding a sack.

"I'll save you some," he promised.

"Don't bother."

I bagged the pack and extended its handles. He took them between his yellowed teeth. Straightening up with a pelvic thrust, he looked to the door. I showed him out.

❀   ❀   ❀

It took all of an hour for word to spread that the Dutchman was gone for the afternoon.

At ten past three, a crowd of Feeders shuffled in with bags and satchels. They mobbed the till, gazing my way. "Hey, Charlie," one said. "Is it true that—"

I spared him. "Yeah. Go on."

They blew apart, whooping and hollering, into the aisles, all the way back . . .

One of them grabbed a box of diapers, claiming his cousin went through five pairs a day power-squatting free weights at the public gym. Another stocked up on Dura-flame logs, determined to fire up the Desmon's hearth. A pair of ghouls raided the deli, digging into the case themselves . . . The rest, of course, went straight for the beer, veering only to raze the chip rack.

After a minute, some toothless scrub in soiled moon gear hobbled over. "Hey, Chuck—you got any flares?"

"Flares? For what?"

"Cuz!" He dribbled. "I wanna shoot them hammers so bad I can taste it. We're never gonna get any sleep, no how."

A roar of agreement swept the floor.

"Yeah, it's true," I concurred. "But no flares."

He lingered, dejected, hands in both pockets. Then, perplexed: "What are you *listening* to?"

"This?"

"Yeah, *that . . .*"

"It's from *The Ring of the Nibelungen*."

"The *who*?"

"It's a opera, idiot!" someone else barked. "What do *you* care? Shut up and help me."

They bagged some Duraflames, then turned to leave. "Thanks a lot, Charlie. See ya later. *Maybe*."

The rest finished up and approached the counter. "How 'bout cigarettes?"

"Yeah—tobacco!"

They all wanted smokes . . .

I doled out a carton of Winston Lights. Like feeding piranhas—panic, a scrapfest . . .

They left in a flurry, pleased as sin. I stared out the window, watching them go . . . Over the walk. Across the lot. Past the hammers. Into the Desmon . . .

＊　＊　＊

I remained in a trance all afternoon. Business was slow on account of the weather. It was mostly a matter of regulating plunder: the tramps got their cold cuts, the Mexicans their Heineken, and all exact change went into my pocket. Otherwise I drifted, staring at the wall and sticking with NPR at all costs.

When the Dutchman returned at a quarter to four, the entire store was in disarray . . . Prokofiev blaring at top volume. The beer unstocked, coffeepot empty. Me at the till, chain-smoking Merits, gulping down eggnog and picking my nose . . . It was all he needed to blow his lid. Here it came . . .

"CHARLES!" he screamed. "Turn off that music! What have I told you about the radio? And how many times will I catch you smoking? It's incorrigible! Get out of here! Unload the car!"

I left the till, bound for shit. Forty beans on. There's always a way . . .

❊   ❊   ❊

At four-thirty, I was back in the stockroom. The Dutchman came in, clearly displeased. "Em-ah, Charles! There's a . . . *person* . . . to see you."

I looked up. "Who?"

"How should I know the answer to this question?" he snapped. "A 'friend,' no doubt. Very dirty."

Tinsel.

I dropped my price gun and walked out the door. He was there by the register, guzzling Yoo-Hoo.

"I'm not finished," I whispered. "Piss off."

"What?"

"I said *split*! The Hague's on a tear."

"Okay." He left.

I returned to the stockroom.

❊

An hour later Hanz was back, only this time on egg-shells. Something had jarred him. "A visitor," he said, more cautious than snide.

I followed him out, pausing in the hall. I knew what was coming. The terror commenced.

I rounded the corner. There she was ... In solid black—upright, indomitable ... Conversing with Hanz. Skirting the till. Nodding and smiling. Heading my way...

A voice in the back of my head taunted: *Imagine making love to* that?

Which, of course, I couldn't. Not for a second. She would've *destroyed* me. I wouldn't last a minute. Shit, I wouldn't *want* to ...

I wouldn't want to soil her.

She reached the hall, stepped in and kept coming. I tripped on a crate while backing away. She pushed us through, then closed the door, relaxed with a sigh and rolled her eyes. "This is a horrible man, this Dutchman!"

I stood there—gaping, stricken, useless.

"I would never want to work for such a person." Shaking her head, she checked me out. "Are you okay?"

I couldn't respond—couldn't figure out where to stand, how to breathe.

"Should I take that as no?" she asked.

"No." *Jesus.* "YES!" *Fuck.* "Everything's fine, but— Had a good day ..."

＊

Here it went. . . .

She turned away, scanning the room. The floor was a
mess. I *had* to say something.

"So how did you manage to" — *e³#!*e³* — "get past him?"

She came back, grinning. "I told him I was your lawyer. You'll excuse my saying, but given your appearance, it
seemed appropriate. How *are* you feeling?"

"Good." *Right.* "Well as can . . ." *Fractured.*

"I'm sorry?"

"FINE!" *Not, I* — " —mean, after . . ." *Damn it!* "Better
than when this morning, I felt . . ."

Jesus fucking shit freak . . .

"Good." She held out a plastic sack. "Sorry I'm early,
but we have dinner reservations in twenty-five minutes."

"*Dinner* reservations?"

"Yes," she said. "A place called the Promenade."

"The *Promenade?*"

"Right. You've heard of it?"

"Well, I've" — *Crazy* — "seen it, but never been" —
doomed — "inside" — *without a chauffeur* — "Really, it's swank,
like —" *Pooh-bah Centrale.* "The swankest in town . . ."

"And what does that mean?" she asked.

"It means —" *@#$%¢e³*.* "'Scuse, I —" *Shit!* "Means:
<u>Fri</u>day night at the Promenade looks like a scene from *The
Godfather.* Not with *us*, you won't . . ."

"Nonsense." Relaxing. "It's simply a matter of proper
dress." She looked to the sack. "Try that on."

I peered inside: tissue, plastic—a gabardine Armani...

"What?" I flinched. "You didn't have to rent this. I've got a suit of my own—back home."

"Yes, and I'm sure it's beautiful, too." She laughed. "I'd love to see it. One day ... However, right now we're running late. You'll have to settle for this. Okay? And no one *rented* it, Charlie. It's yours."

I looked down, gaping: she'd *bought* these? @#$%¢&%@. The jacket alone must've cleared six bills. And the pants, shoes, suspenders, a tie ...

This woman was out of her goddamned mind.

Beautiful, generous, bright, refined—a telltale smash in her own right, maybe—but clearly short on common sense. What else would explain her being *here*?

Again it hit: the *Terror*. Ungodly: locked to the floor with a stick up my ass and both knees on the fold, squirming, wretched ...

Already, I suffered in dealing with women, but this took ineptitude, no, this took full-on drag-me-out-back-with-Slim's-bitch *buffoonery* to whole new levels ... I pictured it now: impaled on a hillside, calling for the angels of mercy to end it—knifed and defiled to every extremity, half of Philth Town over the moon ...

"Look," she broke in, "if I have to tell you one more time, I'll do it myself."

I flew to the john, slammed the door and huddled in a corner, terrified, gasping . . .

The night before, three cans shy of infernal disgrace, I'd drifted away. Now God's gift to humanity ordered my person on threat of violation . . .

There should've been a law against such mindfucks.

"Have you been to New York?" she asked through the door.

"What?" I choked.

"New York. Have you been there?"

"New York City?" *No, the* state, *moron.* "Of course! I mean—yeah, it's a hundred miles up the road." *She really needs a mile count.* "*Yes,* I've been there!"

"Did you like it?"

An air horn tore from my throat.

"Excuse me?" she said.

What does she *want*?

"Charlie?"

"Sorry, I'm—" *Drop it!* "What's the . . ." *Fucking—*". . . question?"

"Do you *enjoy* New York?"

"*Gwoalk!*"

"Is that yes?"

"Uh-<u>HUH</u>!"

Her footsteps tapped across the floor. Pacing, she was. Quiet, reflective. Then: "If so, come visit sometime."

Right. Visit. Let's wait on that . . . If, by chance, following dinner, the offer stands, then we'll talk . . . Hell, if you make it through fifteen minutes of Greetz and me in the holy fuckin' Promenade, then yes, take me home to cuff in the cellar. But for now, get real . . .

"There's a guest room in my flat."

What's the MATTER with this girl?

"Where do you live?" I managed to squeeze.

"Uptown, sadly. I was transferred last year." The footsteps halted. "Are you getting dressed?"

"Huh?" *Yeah, shake a leg.* "Sure, I'm—" *Liar.* "Getting there." *At least make some noise . . .*

I rustled the bag around on the floor. Bent over. Coughed. Veered to one side. A line of spray cans fell from the toilet. Everywhere, clanging. "I'm coming!" *Goddamnit . . .*

I stiffened, braced for the walls to cave in.

Don't move. Don't speak. Don't think. Don't breathe.

"So what about London?" she asked.

"What—London, England?" *No—London, Arkansas, fuckhead*—what's wrong with *you?* "You *do* mean the one in Britain?" *Kill me.*

"Yes." She lilted. "That's the one."

"No, then, no—I've never—" *Really?* "—been."

"Oh." Disappointed. "Pity. Perhaps you should go sometime."

"Why?"

I sensed it coming at once.

"They'd love you there." She laughed again, but this time—*after* a day on the town with Greetz—as though in commiseration. "Are you getting ready?"

"No! I can't seem to"—*fasten the noose*—"almost."

I grabbed the Armani and hung it from a peg. It didn't look real. Felt like silk. The sleeve tag's figure confirmed as much. As in: you could feed an entire town—and not the proverbial third-world hunger pit, but *right here at home* . . .

"Take off the bandage while you're in there," she said. Her footsteps resumed. "And wash your face."

I did as she ordered, huffing and wheezing, out of the rags and into the finery—wishing we could (somehow) leave the door between us for a while—set up a phone, a PO box, the Pony Express, telegraph, smoke signals . . . With a little more time, so long as I wasn't expected to *look* her square in the face, I might emerge from this debilitated stupor, regain my composure, come into form . . .

But time was one luxury she wasn't affording me: the longer I stalled, the worse it got.

Biting the bullet, I opened the door. She was there by a soup rack, back turned, pivoting.

"I can't tie the tie," I announced.

She turned. "Somehow that doesn't surprise me. Sit."

I sat down. She did the rest—straightened the collar, wrapped my skull, knotted the tie—everything short of thumbing me grapes. I didn't even move . . .

"All right." She nodded. "Stand."

I got up. She brushed off my shoulders and backed off, satisfied. "How do you say . . . 'Woman killer'?"

"Lady-killer?"

"*Lady*-killer. You look like a lady-killer." She picked up her bag and took my arm. "Quickly, now . . ."

I hit the floor, a new animal: a rogue hybrid of Willie Horton and Casanova with Garbo in tow. The Dutchman's expression was priceless, eternal. The fallen despot.

So much for my job.

She hustled me out the door to a car. "Get in!" she pointed.

In shock, I complied.

She walked around, got behind the wheel . . .

French, all right.

She drove like a maniac.

THE
OTHER HALF

We reached the hotel to find Tinsel outside—his collar up-turned, face clean-shaven, hair slicked back with two quarts of gel—pacing the walk in a suit of his own. There was no way around it: he looked like a pimp: a third-rate, back-alley, car-thieving love broker straight off the boulevard and down from the screen.

Now it was my turn to laugh . . .

Four weeks earlier, Greetz had outright *flaunted* his refusal to visit a Laundromat, opting instead to torch his rags in an empty lot then make for Goodwill . . . Now, in contrast, here stood Wonderboy—he who wore his filth like a battle flag, who upheld squalor as some kind of ethos, who'd once been ejected from his own gig when the club owner took him for freeloading street trash—here stood Tinsel, the Sultan of Crust, squeaky-clean in a sharkskin Hilfiger, which, despite being mussed around the edges, would remain just that: a thousand-dollar dinner suit.

His embarrassment was evident. He couldn't even *look* at me. The upturned collar and dangling shirttails were simply an attempted diversion from the fact that Louise had succeeded in what no man-of-woman-born had ever thought possible: she'd *cleansed* the Anarchist. She'd told him point-blank to bathe or get out. "Your smell is unnecessary," she said. "I can *taste* it."

Whereupon Tinsel, of course, fired back—but only succeeded in stalling fate. Louise had no interest in arguing the point. Her basic concern lay with breathing clean air. When pressed on the matter, she stared him down with a look that proceeded from narrow to chilling. And thereby, shaken, outclassed and overpowered, he slunk to the can and actually *did* it. He took a bath. With *soap*, to boot . . . And no smart-ass slickster routine would now cover for it.

To think I'd been worried about him railing *me* . . .

❖   ❖   ❖

Our opening moments at the Promenade were spent in a darkened foyer, behind drawn curtains . . . Apparently, despite our improved appearance, problems remained: still too much goatboy bleeding through—especially with me, given my bandage. The hostess glared as though to imply that we'd missed the kitchen doors just up the block. In the end, however, it wasn't pushed. Armani prevailed—or, if not, then our chaperone. None of these fools would cross paths with Louise. Louise, in essence, *exuded* wealth.

To our left, an image of Tony Bennett appeared in a doorway, drawing its curtain. A wave of light and the steady hum of conversation spilled over his shoulders. He beckoned us thither. Louise took the lead. We followed along, into the vortex . . .

From every side, it bowled us over: statues, tapestries, arches, a stage . . . Waiters in stride, busboys careening . . . Food piled up in gluttonous mounds . . . A crooner in white at a baby grand . . . The vaporous tang of top-shelf cosmetics . . . Everywhere, shimmering, dense, panoramic: an onslaught of all things bright and bountiful — pearls and platinum, saffron and silk, frivolity, expenditure, excess, *indulgence* . . .

Tinsel fell over the first chair in view. I skirted him, seized with a grand mal hot flash. Together, we trailed Louise like two village thieves being whipped down a five-mile gauntlet . . .

Along the way, a carcass rolled by. A shrunken apple lolled out of its mouth . . . Or was that the ass? . . . I couldn't tell — the slab had been charred to smoldering gristle . . . The waiters marooned it a table over. Cries of approval went up: "Fantastic!" — declared by a Carmen Miranda in sequins — that wasn't a *fruit basket* on her head? — and a statesman — her husband? — His Corpulence, chortling — calling for gin with a Westminster accent — Billy the Scamp between them, sulking, fed up with travel and dining abroad — and finally, the Princess, Daddy's Angel (her birthday, they said), pointing to a balloon: "Daddy, Daddy!" she called. "Look at the balloon, Daddy! It looks like Jupiter!" (CHEW-PIH-TAH.) "If *that's* what Jupiter looks like, Daddy, then *I* want to go there!"

❉

The images rolled:

His Corpulence, stopped up with bratwurst and Limburger, tearing the shaft on a filthy commode; Carmen, beneath that fertile basket, unveiled as a ravenous, candlewax vixen; Billy the Scamp and Daddy's Angel sold into slavery, penned in a sweatshop—and last, all four of them hopelessly lost on a public bus in the Glokland projects . . .

That did it.

Following the Skullcap debacle, I'd sworn off the grog for weeks to come. And I'd *meant* it, damn it. I was on the wagon—for *real* this time. Detail and all . . .

However, I hadn't anticipated *this*. For the first few moments, I couldn't even *see* straight: crippled with visions of sprawling headlong, wiping out tableloads, ruining whole lives . . . Fortunately, Greetz was no better off: that pall of captive agony shadowed him. Both of us forded the grotesquerie, drowning out of element and going down fast.

Louise picked up on it right away. She ordered two bottles the moment we sat. A busboy nodded and tripped off, grinning. He seemed to be gone for seventeen years. On return, he slipped to my side of the table and presented each label, seeking my approval. I looked up, confused. *Yeah, that's fine—what do you want from me? OPEN the damn thing!*

He popped the cork and poured out a splash. I didn't understand. Why me? Why the smile? *Why do vampires always go for dark meat?*

"You're supposed to test the wine," said Louise.

Test the wine? Like I'm gonna refuse . . .

I slammed it.

There. Was that all right? Now — fill us up and go away. And get rid of Jupiter girl while you're at it.

"Is it to your *satisfaction,* sir?" the busboy schmoozed.

"Yes, it's to my godda —"*Steady.* ". . . I . . ." *Shit.* "YES!" *Damn it.* "POUR!"

Maybe this wasn't so bad after all. Everyone else was abusing the waiters. That much, at least, I *could* do.

❊   ❊   ❊

We downed the first bottle before *thinking* about the menu. Quality aside, it didn't help . . . Behind us, a troupe of southern belles sat chewing the cud over lime-green daiquiris. Farther on, the crooner brayed "If I Only Had a Heart," à la Liberace. Elsewhere, a pack of inebriated stockbrokers frothed and whinnied to their own emissions. And last, two gremlins in spandex took to the stage with a lewd contortionist act.

There's only so far the bottle can go.

Louise appeared to understand. She waited patiently, scanning the floor, as we gulped and slobbered glass after goblet. *Christ, this wine . . .* In stolen glances — *skip the meal —* I took in her profile — *wheel out four more racks of this —* and started to wonder how old she was, how long she'd been here — *twenty-nine years? —* on earth, among us. *Thirty-three, maybe? . . .* God only knew.

Somewhere between womanhood and life eternal.

Eventually, Tinsel came up for air. "Nic fit," he grumbled. "Give me a smoke."

I tossed him my pack. He lit up and puffed, gazing around in mute distress.

After a minute, he tapped his ash in a tray. A tiny man appeared to replace it. Setting a clean tray on top of our own, he removed the pair and lay down a third. Then he backed off and returned to the wall. The new tray sat there, gleaming in the candlelight.

Tinsel, in shock: "Did you *see* that, Chuck?" He gawked, marveling. Again: "Did you *see*? It's like charming a snake. Here—you try!"

"No." I held up my hands. "Get away."

"All right, all right," he huffed. "Jeez. I'll do it myself."

"*Don't,*" I warned him.

"What's wrong with you?"

"You'll give them *ideas.*"

He spat. "Ideas. Watch me make this monkey scoot." He tapped his ash.

Nothing happened.

Clearing his throat, he shifted, annoyed. Another tap. Still no good.

The tiny man was fighting a sauce cart.

Coughing, Tinsel tried again—just for the record.

It wasn't to be.

"I guess I'm a one-hit wonder," he said.

"No, you're not," Louise assured him. "You just have to get the feel for it. Here—give me your cigarette." She took the butt. "It's all a matter of sitting tall." Arching her back,

she peered around. The stage act swelled to a sudden crescendo. Every busboy hovered, spellbound . . . Winking,
Louise tapped her ash.

They hit from every side at once. I nearly got up and
ran for cover. Our table was sealed off. The hostess came
by. Along with a waiter and Tony Bennett . . . Swarming,
they gave us new ashtrays, bread, a bowlful of olives and
wine all around. Then, just as suddenly, vanished again—
back to their stations and faulty sauce carts.

"Jesus!" Greetz, blown out in the aftermath. "How did
you *do* that?"

"Don't worry," she said. "You'll get it. Soon."

"Hell NO! I don't *want* to get it."

"Too bad." She passed him the butt. "I have to make a
phone call now. Excuse me." She got up and walked.

The Anarchist turned, out of his mind. "Take this,
man—before they come back."

"Don't look at me."

"Don't look at *you*?" He pinched the butt like a mur-
der weapon. "It's *your* smoke."

"Yeah, but *your* idea. *You* deal with it."

Trembling: "Smash it under the table!" he pleaded.

"No."

"Come on! *Help* me!"

The belles looked over in sudden alarm. Greetz slid
down the length of his backrest. The butt kept burning.

"Eat it," I hissed.

"What?"

"*Eat* it! There's no other way."

"I can't—it's lit!" He blanched. "*You* eat it!"

"No."

"Yes, goddamnit!"

"Listen," I said. "The ashtray's out. The floor's off-limits. You'll never make the toilet . . . I told you not to give them ideas."

He glowered, seething, rabid, crestfallen. If looks could kill, that would've been it.

But the clock was still ticking. Sands in the hourglass. The butt hung top-heavy, ash set to go. With a final grimace, he opened wide, crushed the cherry and swallowed down.

❈   ❈   ❈

The menu.

I'd never heard of these dishes. I could barely make out what *language* the damn thing was written in. All I could read for certain were the prices, and the hors d'oeuvres exceeded my tab at Maxine's.

Louise reappeared. "Have you decided?" she asked.

No, we haven't decided. LOOK at us.

"Maybe I can make a suggestion," she offered.

Yes, please do.

"The goat-cheese salad should be good. Also the lamb. Or the brochettes."

"I was just thinking about that lamb," said Tinsel.
Right — like hell you were, Greetz . . .

"Okay." She nodded. "And afterward?"
"Afterward?"
"No, pardon me — " she caught herself. "I meant before-
hand. The appetizer . . ."
"Appetizer?"

Two courses?

This girl must be a cop . . .

A waiter appeared, all schmaltz and cordiality. "Good
evening." He bowed.

Here goes . . .

"Give me the salad!" Tinsel barked.
The waiter recoiled, taken aback. "The Polomanian
salad with the *crème de chèvre,* sir?"
"Right. But hold the cream. And don't call me 'sir.'"
"I'm sorry?"
"No cream. Just the salad."
"'Cream,' sir?"
"No cream, no 'sir'!" Tinsel knocked his fork from the
table. It flew. "Shit!" He went after it, slamming his head.
"*Uurrgg.*" He bobbed up, wincing in pain. "Listen," he moaned.
"Don't mind me. The cream's fine. Everything's fine. Especially
with cream, and whatever else . . . Lamb. Give me the lamb!"

The waiter tugged one ear, perplexed. "Would you not prefer the salad first?"

"No, all at once. Just give me the cream—*along* with the chicken. At your leisure."

"Chicken, sir?"

"CHICKEN!" screamed Tinsel. "Is there a problem with that?"

"No! Heavens, no problem at all. It's just that I thought you asked for the . . . lamb."

"Chicken, lamb—whatever, same shit! Both. With cream, at once . . . And more wine!"

"More wine, sir?"

"*Yes*, more wine! Don't tell me I'm flagged already?"

"*Flagged*, sir?" The waiter shook, by now setting standards in infinite patience. "But of course not. I'm simply asking after your preference."

Tinsel looked over as though to say, *What's wrong with this guy?* Then, worse still: "My *preference*? What is this?"

"No, that's not—" Regrouping, flustered. "Would you not prefer a particular *label* of wine. Sir."

"Oh. *That* preference . . . I don't know. Red, white." Greetz slumped forward, crumbling. "Please, just—bring me a beer . . ."

To his credit, the waiter seemed prompted to sympathy.

On the other hand, he now had orders for lamb and chicken to be delivered alongside a salad—*with*, then without, then *with again* nebulous goat cream, and finally, carte

blanche in the wine cellar, quantity, label and type unspeci-
fied. All from one order. And there were still two *more* of us.

He swung by Louise as some kind of detour. Then got
to me—downtown Kinshasa. Optimum precaution: "Good
evening," he said. "May I take your order?"

"Give me the croquettes. And *red* wine. Excuse—" I
shot from the table, johnward-bound.

"But sir!" he called.

Too late. Keep moving. His Corpulence. Gremlins. A
busboy, Jupiter . . . Finally, the stall door: through and in,
empty—down on all fours to the rim of a urinal.

Phase one was over. The program, blown. All-time
record lows indeed.

Tinsel and I were no better off in the castle than back
on Glokland Row. We belonged in a mine shaft—roasting
possum and fungal discharge. Mole folk. Terminal.

I thought about slipping away right then—out the door
and back to Our Lady to wallow in potting soil, stick myself, bleed . . .

Or maybe I'd take my meal in here—little table in the
corner, Wet Naps, candlelight. Dinner for one at the porcelain altar . . .

But that wouldn't do. They'd call me a malcontent. Or
worse yet—depraved: *The Watcher in the Water Closet* . . .

❃

Piss on that. No more retreat. Besides, I couldn't leave her with *him* . . .

I crawled to my feet. Walked to the mirror. Picked up a hot towel. Dabbed my neck . . .

For the first time all night, the Armani stood out . . . Everything to it . . . Shit, I looked *fine* . . . Sure, I'd worn suits for the union, on occasion—but none like *this* . . . Nothing even close. Louise had been right: I looked like a *lady-killer* . . .

From out of nowhere, back in the game.

I pitched the hot towel. Strutted, flouncing. Pulled a split, hopped up. *Suave* . . . Out came the air guitar . . . Rocking the nation, the Fractured Bachelor . . . A Townshend windup over the trash can—a flying kick to the hot-towel bin . . . God *damn*, but he's smooth! . . . Check him out! *Vicious!*

Squaring off with number one: *All right, Chuck—remind these fools that giants walk the earth.*

I tucked the bandage, straightening up. Blew my reflection a kiss. Turned. Strode out the door. Clipped a waiter. Pie on the floor.

Jesus fuck.

Again running, the Emperor Jones—bane of existence, scorn of the ilk . . .

I reached our table, crashed into place.

Tinsel, distracted. "What happened to you?"

"Nothing!" I blurted.

"Problems with the toilet?"

"No!"

They stared.

"What's happening *here*?" I turned it around. "Speaking French, haven't you?"

"Yes," said Louise. "How did you know?"

"I can smell it." *GONG!* "I mean, *heard* it." *Shit.*

Wincing, Tinsel: *Swift, Charlie . . .*

"Sorry," I kept on, "what were you saying?"

"She was just talking 'bout Zelda," he murmured.

"Yeah?" I snapped to, grabbing my wine. "What's the story?" Guzzling down.

"Our friend paid a visit to Sunshine this morning. Bought nine of her photos. The *big* ones, you know?"

I choked. "Pardon." Wiping my chin with one sleeve. "That's good!"

"Well, *yeah*, that's good. *Saved our ass* is more like it."

"It had nothing to do with your ass," said Louise. "We would have bought the photos, regardless. Our needs were specific, and Miss Deeds was our only contact. Circumstance delayed foreclosure, that's all . . . However, if I were you – *especially* you" – she motioned to Greetz – "I'd keep my distance for a little while. She's going to need some time."

"Of course! Like Charlie said: I would've killed us both by now . . . She's got time." He went for an olive, seemingly satisfied. Then, as afterthought, smirking: "But she *will* get over it. We all know that."

"What makes you so sure?"

He gobbed the pit. "Cuz she loves me too much," he drooled. "Can you blame her?"

❁   ❁   ❁

Our appetizers arrived—braided swirls of meat and foliage smothered in gruel.

My system yawned like a sunbaked sponge to a downpour of long-depleted nutrients. Soon my head began to clear. My sphincter retracted. It boggled the mind . . . People all over the world were *eating.* The things I could do on three squares daily . . .

Slowly, I drifted out of Quasimodo and (somewhat) into form. By the end of the first course, I was comfortably certain this girl was not, in fact, a cop. By the start of the second, the tables around us were even beginning to appear less suspect.

This at last gave Louise a chance to tell us something about herself. Which, it turned out, was overdue, as until then, I'd been under false assumptions. She wasn't a photographic investor at all. She was a field correspondent for the French media. Her being in Philth Town was purely incidental; some producer had arranged this two-day stop for the purpose of securing Zelda's work—a series of photos detailing police brutality during a public convention. Beyond her roll as temporary messenger, Louise herself wasn't in on the project. Her own destination lay farther east—so far east she had to fly west: some hilltop village in coastal New Guinea where hundreds of cheese-goat rebels were locked in a heated standoff with government troops . . .

"Cheese goats?" Tinsel blurted. "Hold on! Where in the living hell is New Guinea?"

"In the South Pacific. Above Australia."

"Above Aus*tralia*?" He dropped his fork. "What are you talking?" Losing his cool: "Come on! Let's have it! What gives with these goats?"

"It's not the goats, you ass. It's the ranchers, the land-owners."

"Fine. What's the story?"

"We don't know yet."

"Well, can't you find out?"

"By flying there—yes."

"What about the phone?"

"Communications are down."

"And the consulate?"

She laughed: "You haven't been to New Guinea."

At first I assumed she was putting us on. Cheese goats, rebels, the South Pacific—what came next, *Voyage to Kunlun*? . . . No, surely she spoke in jest.

Yet soon her delivery bore out the contrary. Indeed, she dealt with such stories by trade. "Global human inter-est," they called it. For seven years she'd been working the field—*which*, in essence, appeared to revolve around prob-ing the depths of male imbecility. Stateside alone, her back-log included: snake handling in Georgia, cockfighting in the Southwest, drug abuse in Alaskan canneries, independent militias in Texas . . .

"Haven't you had any problems?" I asked.

"Problems?" she said. "Such as?"

"I mean, these assignments of yours—aren't some of them a bit, you know . . . *dangerous*?"

Yes," she replied.

I scratched my head. "Well . . ."

She waited, then casually offered: "How do I avoid being raped or killed?"

"We *could* start there."

"Yes, I thought so." She'd done this before. "While traveling in numbers—say, six or more—*with* press badges, there's rarely a problem. However, at times 'the badge must come off.' And you can't always count on numbers. Therefore—"

"You pack heat!" Tinsel enthused.

"Well, that's one way of putting it."

"Right on. Ever used it?"

"What?"

"Ever smoked someone?"

"No!"

"But you *have* used it."

She hesitated. "Sort of . . ."

"What does that mean?"

"Well . . ."

"Come on!" yelled Greetz.

"It's hard to explain." She shook her head. "Just something that happened a long time ago."

"In Texas?"

"No, Gabon."

"Where's that?"

"West Africa. Having trouble with geography tonight?"

"No more than you with your English," he snapped.

"She's much better-spoken than you," I said.

"True," he admitted. "Why *is* that, anyway?"

"My father was from Quebec," she answered. "And you?"

"My father?"

"Your French. Where'd you learn it?"

"Oh, that . . . Same person to blame for this haircut— my mother."

"So that's the story," she said. "I thought a lawn mower fell on your head."

"No, *that* was my father. Fat bastard."

"Right," I cut in. "What about Gabon?"

"Yeah!" called Tinsel.

She looked away, embarrassed. "It's nothing."

"We've been through this part already."

"Okay."

"Did someone attack you?"

"Actually"—she cuffed her brow—"someone tried to *eat* us."

Tinsel: "EAT you?"

Me: "What?"

"SHIT!" Together.

"I know." Louise. "But you must understand—I was very young. Courageous, perhaps. But young. Naive."

"What were you doing?" I asked. "When it happened."

"Filming a ceremony. Things went wrong."

Tinsel slobbered, gnashing mutton. "Hell *yeah*, sounds like—"

"And you call that 'nothing'?" I asked her.

"Well, I suppose it *was* bad."

"Yet apparently" — Greetz — "you haven't learned much since."

"Excuse me?" she said.

"I'm talking about last night, Toots."

"What about it?" I asked.

He looked to me. "I'm saying: no flower like that belongs in the projects without a Beretta revolver, right?"

"Beretta doesn't make revolvers," said Louise.

He turned back, flinching. "I meant Perazzi."

"Perazzi doesn't make *pistols*." She laughed. "And lose the 'flower.'"

"All right, all right! My point was: you, in particular, should not be wandering Baltimore Avenue alone, after dark. This place can be nasty as anything in Africa."

"I've heard that," she said.

"Really?" I asked.

"Yes. This town's reputation precedes it."

"As what, a port of extremes?" I guessed.

She looked over. "Actually, in those terms exactly. Why, is that common knowledge?"

"No, just the truth," I said.

"Yes?"

"Hm."

"Why?" she asked.

"Because it's the only spot where you thaw out from deep freeze into a heat stroke."

"And what?" she prodded. "No in between?"

"Well, there's Kensington," I said.

"Kensington?"

"Yes, have you been there?"

"No," she said.

"You should go sometime."

She smiled. "Nice try."

"Can't blame me."

"I don't. But what about Kensington?"

Greetz: "It's a hole! What does this have to do with cheese goats?"

"Yeah," I concurred. "Cheese goats!"

"I already told you," she said, "we don't know yet."

"Sounds like you might need help," cracked Tinsel. "Why not take Charlie along as bag boy?" He shot back, laughing. "Can't you see it—the Half-breed scrappin' through jungle paddies, dodging pitchforks, tripping on cheese goats. Ha!" He slapped the table. "Damn, I can hear it now: *Just don't drop the camera, boy!*"

"Actually, I was thinking about *you*," said Louise.

He looked up. "Me? For what?"

"Herding cattle through minefields. You interested?"

"Shit." He snatched a potato from her plate. "I'm more of a sharpshooter."

"Not here, Greetz . . ."

He blew me off, thumbing the spud over top of a butter knife, then drew back . . . It clipped an apple in Carmen's basket. She whirled, gasping.

"*Oh!*" I jolted.

"It hit her!"

"Don't look."

We stared at the table, trying not to laugh.

"Nice shot," said Louise.

"Is she looking?"

"Yes."

"Just take it easy," I whispered.

"Nice shot."

❊   ❊   ❊

With the downing of a third bottle, things fell together.

Greetz continued playing devil's advocate, I sat nursing my wine, at ease, while Louise just kept getting better and better — too good to be true, it appeared, yet so . . . The fact that she'd taken our company now seemed less outlandish. In fact, it made sense. No one who dealt with cheesegoat rebels would spend two days holed up in her room. No media dinners or somber affairs with unknown contacts would cut it, either. She would need movement, some chance, a gamble. She'd relish the prospect of comic relief. Hence, her decision to bring us here . . .

By and by, she obliged our requests for several correspondence tales. One in particular busted me up, though you had to be there. Suffice it to say: *Pitchfork Brigade of Brazilian Farmers Loses Flock to Vampire Bat* . . . Despite the *terror*, her recap left me with visions of hopping a freighter to Reno.

The topics rolled from travel to music, then onward to zoos and, thereby, wildlife. Louise, yielding to Greetz so as not to monopolize, soon wound up in a death match.

"Who you got between a tiger and a grizzly?" He popped the question at random.

"A tiger and a grizzly?" she said. "In combat?"

"Yeah, in a thirty-foot cage."

She considered. Then: "The tiger, I guess. Though my heart's with the grizzly."

"That's what Chuck says. But what about a grizzly and a polar bear?"

"The grizzly."

"The grizzly."

"The *polar* bear, fools!"

"A grizzly would kick a polar bear's ass!" I said.

"No doubt," Louise agreed.

"All right." He moved on. "A goose and a pelican?"

"The goose."

"The goose."

"No argument there. But a coot and a thrush?"

"No contest." Louise. "Try a monkey and a lemur."

"The monkey," I decided.

"What's a lemur?" asked Greetz.

"Never mind," she continued, searching. "Let's see . . ."

"A yak and a womp rat!" Tinsel motioned.

"Forget that," I said. "A badger and a mongoose."

Greetz: "The badger."

"A mongoose." Louise.

He slapped the table. "You're just being contrary!"

"And?" She laughed. "That *bothers* you?"

"Okay," I cut in. "A rat and a king snake."

"The king snake," she answered.

"The rat!" he insisted.

"*Who's* being contrary?"

"SLAG ONE, baby."

"Charlie?"

"The king snake."

"Your mother!" said Greetz.

Louise: "What about a boxer and a goat?"

"The goat," I answered.

"The boxer, for Jesus!"

"I would have to go with the goat," she settled it. "But where does that leave us with a boar and a pit bull?"

Greetz: "The pit bull."

"The boar!" I yelled.

"What would *you* know, Virgin?"

"From *pit* bulls, Low Rent."

"Settle down, boys . . ."

Tinsel: "All right then—Lennon and McCartney?"

"That's *rude*!"

"Okay—a Firebird and a Pinto?"

She looked away.

"Who *cares*?" I said. "Besides, you can't fit the two in a cage."

"Then Chaplin and Keaton."

"That's not *fair* . . ."

"All right. Fatty and Lloyd."

"Arbuckle."

"Yes."

"Fatty unanimous!"

Down the hatch, we drank to Fatty.

"A jackal and a coyote." Greetz resumed.

"Draw," I said.

"The coyote," Louise.

"A collie and a bobcat?" Tinsel again.

"That's *lame*," I said.

"Then a croc and a hippo . . ."

"The croc."

"The croc."

"Jaws and Orca."

"Orca."

"Jaws."

"Bullshit Jaws!" Tinsel yelled. "Orca destroyed a whole *town* from the water. Jaws can't touch that!"

"Sorry," Louise.

"What did you say?"

"Well, I've never actually *seen* Orca."

"Yeah, that figures."

"Here," I suggested. "SEALs and Delta?"

"Now *that* is lame."

"Sorry," I folded.

"Camacho and Trinidad," Greetz continued.

"Oh! Yeah!" I sat up. "That's tonight!"

"Who you got?"

"Tito."

"How much?"

"Twenty."

"Go *fifty*?"

"You serious?"

"As cancer."

"You're on!"

"Good!" He licked his chops. "Cuz Tito'll suck the canvas in three."

"Uh-huh."

"That's right!" he yelled. "This'll be one quick Mexican fight."

"It's a 'turf war,' fool—not a 'Mexican fight.' And besides, they're both from Puerto Rico."

"Same shit. He's still going down."

Louise, tiring: "I think we've had enough of this game."

"NO!" hollered Greetz. "We're just getting started. Christopher Reeve and Stephen Hawking?"

"That's *terrible!*"

"Yeah."

"Okay," he conceded. "Artaud and Kinski."

"Artaud."

"I suppose."

"Kinski in six!"

Laughing: "*Kinski . . .*"

He bristled. "Fine, then—Alien and Predator!"

"Who?" she said.

"Predator."

"*Why?*" I asked.

"Is that like *The Terminator*?"

"No. But speaking of screen 'droids—" He lifted a finger. "I've got Corollo's itinerary."

"Oh?" I looked up.

"Yeah." He grinned. "They're shooting tomorrow at four A.M. I figure an overhand toss from the roof . . ."

"Why do you hate him so much?" asked Louise.

"*Hate* him?" said Greetz, deferring to me: "How would *you* answer that?"

I shrugged. "Cuz he used to be *good*?"

"But what?" she followed up. "Not anymore?"

We shook our heads.

"And he won't get it back?"

"Unlikely," I said.

"Guaran*teed*!" shouted Tinsel. "Delvin Corollo will never make another decent film in his life! Bank on it, live it, be*lieve* me, I know . . . The *Times* has been blowing sugar up his ass—calling him the greatest living American director—for twenty years now, *fifteen* of which he's pissed away believing it. That's too much time on the wrong track, folks. He'll never get it back. He's beyond recall."

"So then who *is* the greatest living American director?" Louise asked.

"There's no such thing," Greetz declared. "We're talking *cinema* here. The Americans have nothing to do with it."

Touché.

"If you want to make a *real* film," he continued, "you ought to check out what I've got going . . ."

On which he launched into his bank-robbing scheme, always and forever the king of tact.

At first she paid him no special mind. A joke, surely. One more tangent. She couldn't be bothered by aimless yammering now that our night was underway . . .

But as he delved into "sanctuaries"—available hideouts in the event of a manhunt—her look of tranquillity gently ebbed, dissolving to one of puzzled distaste. Further confusion resulted when Tinsel referred to a mystery "getaway driver"—someone equipped with a German luger and "fucking well ready to use it, like Chuck" . . . And once he settled on clear intentions of pulling the job in a Nixon mask, she could bear no more. In jest or nay, his plan was offensive. The shit hit the fan.

Fortunately, it went no further in English. Passions summoned the mother tongue. The two of them flew into battle undubbed, drawing startled looks from every table. I didn't pick up on a word between them, which was better—I didn't want to know. The voice of reason would always lose out when it came to Greetz and his myriad ploys. Of course, Louise didn't realize this and so persisted, just egging him on. They went back and forth, pounding the table, blasting each other, imploring the heavens. I was caught up in praising my lingual restrictions the moment she turned. "Did you *hear* this?"

"Yes," I sighed. "I've heard all about it."

"But—it's *idiotic*!" she said.

"It's *not*!" countered Tinsel. "You'll see. Both of you. Mark my words: I'll be in Acapulco tossing down shots by the time you're done with your cheese goats, honey. Remember, Bonaparte had skeptics, too. And who got the last laugh there?"

She shouted: "Exactly! Wellington!"

"Nooo . . . *before* that!" He grimaced, thrown off. "Hell, you two were made for each other . . . *You*, Miss Chatterley"—facing Louise—"with your hot-pink parasol and bottomless credit line. And *you*"—to me—"of little fucking faith, even worse: an unemployed one-trick pony. And with *that*—" He leaned in, beaming, triumphant. "I'm off to find out what lurks in the water closet."

He got up and made for the john with the most ridiculously overblown ghetto strut ever. We watched him go, not knowing whether to laugh or cry.

Louise, turning: "He's a fool if he thinks that'll work."

"I know," I conceded, embarrassed. "But you really ought to save your breath. You're only encouraging him."

"But—" Looking away, she allowed it to register. "Just seems that someone should *tell* him, that's all."

"He's *been* told," I said. "A thousand times. You can't talk sense into Greetz. Forget it."

She came back around. "You're not thinking about *joining* him, are you?"

"Joining him?" *Whoa!* "Are you kidding? Jesus, do you know how many bank jobs make it these days?"

"Yes!" She knew exactly. "Less than five percent."

"Right," I assumed. "And Tinsel's involvement *guarantees* this won't be one of them . . . No, don't worry—I won't be joining him. I've got plans of my own."

She shifted. "What kind of plans?"

"Getting out of here." It felt good just saying it.

"What, you mean leaving the city?" she asked.

"That's right."

"And going where?"

"I don't know. Maybe Ghanzi."

"Botswana?"

"Yes."

She considered. "That's a first."

I shrugged. "I've heard it's sunny there."

She nodded. "So why don't you take him with you?"

"*With* me?" I twitched. "Listen, no disrespect intended, but *he's* half the reason I'm leaving at all."

"Ah!" That got her. "I *have* been wondering."

"What?"

"Well, you'll excuse my saying, but the two of you hardly strike me as committed."

"Oh?"

"Yes. I mean, *listening* to it . . . Back and forth. As a by-stander, one can only imagine. There seems to be genuine rancor between you."

I shrugged. "Well, it's not *that* bad. He's just a pain in the ass, that's all."

"Okay." She spoke once I failed to elaborate. "I guess that explains it. *Sort* of."

"Sorry. Put it this way: He's like this town. Again, those extremes . . . When he's *off*, worse than the kiss of death; when he's *on*, the greatest company around. I guess the fact that there's no in between is what holds my attention."

"I see." She nodded. "And that's why you spend your time together?"

"No, not exactly," I backpedaled, jamming. Then: "In fact, that's a whole different question."

"To which you would answer?"

To which I replied, employing a hitherto fail-safe re-frain: "Every time we get together, something happens. That's our chemistry."

"Okay." She sounded more satisfied now. "And where do *you* fit in with that?"

I blinked. "Huh?"

"I mean, what's your part in that 'chemistry'? What's *your* story?"

Hell, I'd never been *called* on it . . .

Slipping: "I don't have a story," I said.

She shook her head. "We all have a story."

I hit my drink to quell the furnace: "Not this time." Which sounded ridiculous . . .

"And that's wrong, too." She frowned, unimpressed. "What I've been hearing is very interesting."

Snapping around: "*What* was that?"

She nodded. "Your friend told me things. This morning."

"Like what?" I demanded. "What did he tell you?"

Pulling no punches, she sallied forth: "He told me you were born in war-torn Saigon—that your mother was, presumably, a Cambodian prostitute; your father, a black American soldier—that at one month of age, you were discovered in a suitcase, floating through the luggage claim at JFK—that neither of your parents were ever located—that an officer named you Charlie as a joke—that you wound up in numerous foster homes and state facilities throughout childhood—that you fell down a flight of stairs last month—'too blown on vodka to find your room' . . . and that now, you live in a dirty hotel, killing rats in the sewers between deli shifts."

Well, there it was.

I had known this woman for less than a day. Yet, counting cards, she'd already seen me: mauled to a pulp, tossing my cookies, bleeding all over her backseat upholstery—rav-

ing deplorable naked by night, fumbling worthless the morning after and slaving the day in a filthy trough: all the grislies
in Technicolor—and *now*, to drive the knife in to the hilt, she
finds out through Greetz that I'm also, dig: an *orphaned whore-
son half-bred refugee / till-bound alcoholic slaghand Bottom-feeder . . .*

What do you do with a label like that—*sell beef to the
Hindus,* as Tinsel would urge?

No, you can't do *shit* with that. Every nail had been
sunk in the coffin . . .

My only remaining dignified option: to leave the table,
hit the john and ram the scurly fucker's snout so far down
the toilet, he'd choke on New Jersey.

"Excuse me." I stood. "I'll be right back."

"Hold it!" She grabbed me. "I'm not done yet."

What, there's more?

She pulled me around, got her leverage, then told—not
asked or implored but *told* me: "Sit down."

I did as she said, fuming.

"You didn't let me finish."

To think I stuck up for him . . .

"Are you listening?" she asked.

No loyalties . . .

"Hello?" she persisted.

"Hm."

"Is that yes?"

I nodded.

"Good," she said flatly. "Because he also told me you're
brilliant."

❧

Boom.

"That life in this place would be pointless without you, and that a fine man . . ." She halted, searching. "A finer man . . ." Giving up: "Something about a fine man in shoes. I didn't quite get it."

I slumped in my chair.

"Do you know what that means?"

"Yeah, yeah . . ."

"Well?" She waited. "Why are you *laughing*?"

I buried my face. "It's 'A finer man never stood in two shoes.'"

"And what's that—a line from Edward the First?"

"No." I peered through my fingers, delirious. "But his name *was* Edward."

She waited for a follow-up that never came. "All right." Exasperated. "*Who* was Edward?"

I went for my goblet with steadied hands. "Edward was the baddest white boy who ever lived. Outside of Zimmerman, of course."

She rolled her eyes. "And *who* was Zimmerman?"

"Zimmerman wrote the greatest rock-and-roll album of all time."

"Oh, my *fff* . . ." Biting her lip, hopelessly lost in my hall of fame. "And what *record* was that?"

Smiling, I said: "It's called *Highway 61 Revisited*."

Ah!" She swept her glass from the table. "I was beginning to think we'd never come around."

"What?" I stammered. "You mean. You *know* it?"

"Of course!" She frowned, insulted. "What do you think I am, *dull*? . . . I just have trouble understanding you some-

times. You have to remember, I only speak *English.*" She held
up her wine. "To the Jokerman, right? And Edward the
white boy! Along with his shoes."

"Cheers."

We toasted.

I drank the health of Bob and Ned with Helen of
Troy.

Hot *ꝺamn*!

Entire lives are justified on lesser moments . . .

Then came Greetz: swaggering out of the john at a
clip, back for more . . . All cock-of-the-walk in his hiked-up
britches, he seemed intent on a class reentry. However, instead of skirting the cake rack, he plowed right into it, square
in the balls . . .

A tray of pastries crashed to the floor. Tinsel went down
with a sickening thud. Louise and I spat wine across the
table . . .

Everyone else fell silent, mortified.

Tony Bennett appeared from the kitchen. Caught un-
awares, he zeroed in: one sharkskin Hilfiger steeped in a
bomb site of custard and chocolate, spewing obscenities. As
with the others, he froze on impact, settling into a paralyzed
trance . . .

Groaning, Tinsel got to his feet, lathered in frosting,
limelit, decrepit. Save for the clamor of rattling cutlery, the
room was quiet as Sunday in Kansas—the waiters as-

tounded, busboys aghast, the crowd, a paler shade of revolted . . . No one stepped forward, no one helped out. They
made him do it all on his own.

He crossed the floor, heading our way. Got to his seat,
plunked down and brushed off. "Well," he grumbled, leering at Carmen. Then, with an air of lofty disdain: "The rich,
Charlie — they are very different from you and me . . ."

❋   ❋   ❋

By half past eight, the place was a zoo — each counter lined
tight with new arrivals. Of the opening crowd, just a handful
of stragglers, along with His Corpulence & Kin, remained.
Everyone else was in from the cold, wafting along in a cos-
metic haze.

The three of us languished, basking euphoric — sealing
cahoots in the din of it all. Greetz on a first-name basis with
our waiter, getting busboys to fetch him loose scraps from
empty tables — Louise between us, nursing a highball, trying to remember the name of some jazz haunt — me to the
left, buried in goblets, halfway through to the promised land.
Everyone else at our beck and call. There seemed to be
nothing we couldn't demand. Barbacks trotting to market
for cigarettes. The hostess presenting us drinks on the house.
The crooner obliging our every request. Even the chef on
hand for introductions. All unfolding beneath the penum-
bra of Louise's Triple-Platinum-Corporate-Exclusive-
MasterCard-for-the-Cream-of-the-Elite, or whatever she
was packing — put a down payment on an F-16 with the
plastic footing *this* bill . . .

❋

A violinist appeared at our table—eyes aglow, bow adrift, coattails skirting the floor in swirls—serenading some bile to Louise . . .

Startled, I reeled in a waiter. "Who *did* this?"

He pointed to a group of snickering brokers huddled in league on an elevated platform.

They'd sent this clown to play for Louise.

They were *lusting* after Louise . . .

"*Give me that goddamned thing!*" I stood, grabbing the fiddle.

"Go get 'em, Breed!"

Over the floor at a furious clip. A wave of panic swept the room. Gasping. Horror. Cries to Jove. Several waiters dodged from my path. Followed by a woman in gold lamé . . . I paid them no mind, just kept on moving—all four brokers, framed in the crosshairs . . .

They saw me coming, called for help. But none was in range. Chickenshit white boys. Reaching the platform, I climbed up the railing, swung over top and dropped to their side. A scream cut the air as I lifted the bow . . .

There *was* one thing Greetz hadn't told Louise.

I bore down with Bartók. "Allegro Barbaro." From out of the skies, plummeting earthbound—every purist's ultimate nightmare: "Massacre of the Elders in D Flat Minor . . ."

One broker spilled his drink on the floor. The others braced to flee for their lives. But none would escape, not with me there—wunderkind rising, terror of men—stewing their goose in defense of *the code*; my lady, her honor, civility, virtue . . .

The Bartók run was fairly brief, but the storm to follow brought time to a standstill . . .

Beginning at the root, I started into a long, discordant ascending crescendo—two steps up, a half back, two more rising, another in retreat—climbing the scale in haphazard increments, dive-bombing octaves in wild swoops, leveling out, then switching keys and delving into a Slavic refrain (root to seventh to second to third) that quickened and intensified from 360 to 420 to a final, overpowering 480 strokes per minute.

I rode that peak for as long as I could, steadily fraying the bow hairs thin, then forcefully adjourned to an augmented sixth for a Parthian shot, one last flurry . . . Ending thus—rocked back on my heels with an elbow jacked to the ceiling fan—would, in theory, leave these snowflakes drifting in a netherworld of unresolved dissonance . . .

You could have blown them over with a table fan.

Given time, one may have picked up on the El rolling by twelve blocks to the north. Likewise, the music of the spheres might have grown to include the hum of prep-room equipment. A pocket watch ticking in somebody's jacket, the tonsular slurs of the petrified brokers, even the rumble of distant traffic could, somehow, drift into audible range

. . . But as it stood, with the gale having lifted in mid-pitch and -course, the silence was total. Those within earshot teetered in flux, lost in an echo, drifting, violated . . .

As for me, the battle was over. No body count needed to verify its outcome. The stockbrokers, all of them, would now settle up and slink away, assassinated, spent castratos . . . My role as cavalier had been played out. All that remained was a fitting exit.

Instead of using the stairs to my left, I climbed back over the platform railing. I'm not sure why—I wasn't really thinking. The gears were still jammed on autopilot.

Only when I turned did reality hit. And then, with a vengeance . . .

Every face. Every table. Every buck, wench and whelp —our hostess, Billy, the tiny man, Carmen—*thunderstruck* with primordial wonder . . . Gazing back, I dropped my guard. The scene resembled a house of wax, with me at center stage, encircled. Cast in stone. Pompeii. The Burghers . . .

Then a response lit out from one corner, though slowly at first, with hesitation: a ponderous clap that, gradually building in pace and resolve, rose unaccompanied. Once on track, it was joined by another. In tandem they spread, gaining momentum. Soon the entire floor was awash from foyer to cake rack and all points between.

I found myself swamped in a standing ovation: torrents of applause from every table—whistles, stomps, calls for an encore. Unanimous praise for the fractured bachelor . . .

Down in front, the Crooner shouted—hands held high, pearly whites gleaming. Behind him, Carmen hiked up a leg and joggled her girth, baying obscenely. Greetz, on his chair, yelled, "That's my brother, goddamnit—my slope jack! That's *my* friend!" Even Tony Bennett stood whooping and hollering, borne from the trenches of endless servility.

I plowed through the mob, back to our table, and sat to a smothering round of praise. His Corpulence sent over a bottle of wine. Some busboys implored me to strike up another. A penguin in cashmere presented his card in hopes that I'd play some wedding in Delaware . . . Suddenly, everyone loved the Half-breed. To hell with Botswana—*this* was home.

Then I caught sight of Louise, gaping: eyes like cake plates, out of the water—completely, *utterly* blown away . . .

All peripherals dropped from the picture. The soundtrack cut, the chatter subsided. I must have ignored a whole slew of requests. I even spaced through a toast to my health. None of it mattered. I'd lost my grounding. There was only me and Louise Gascoygne—Chuck and Helen, Breed and the Beauty—caught in a whirlwind of recognition: she, at last, down from the cross—the ideal given form—to reciprocal common ground—me, torn from the ship of fools and out on parade as royalty born—both of us drifting in spellbound rapture, free-floating, weightless, gone to the world . . . Together, our children would boldly account for three major races of humankind.

✽

Reaching over, she pulled me in. I didn't resist. All Hail Discordia . . .

No one's *ever* kissed me that way.

A burst of applause went up all around us.

Somewhere out there, cities were burning. The Dow was in peril. Floods rocked the coast . . .

None of it mattered—troubles be damned. There was only me and Louise Gascoygne.

BACCHUS

Hours later, Felix Trinidad won a twelve-round decision over Hector Camacho. All three judges at ringside scored the bout for Tito with change to spare. A decent fight, as shutouts go, though one predictably riddled with fouls—a fight that would jettison Felix to stardom, a fight on which Greetz would lose $50, and a fight that would leave all three of us yelling and slamming the countertop at Maxine's . . .

Truly, a fitting continuation—the second of many winds in the dervish.

Onward thence, with Money tending—the Seminole Pops delivering good, countless rounds of Jack and Coke, a dance with Louise to "All of Me"—followed by food at the Taco Hole, then rum and tequila at Danny Gill's and onward to one more scene in the lobby—Greetz in an oil-slicked tutu dug from a pile of trash along Theatre Row, lashing the deskmen for recommending he bathe before coming to breakfast that morning—we wound up back in Louise's suite, all paying tribute to Moon the Loon: Tinsel amok on a mattress in bounds, the top of his head just grazing the ceiling; Louise hopping from couch to recliner, barefoot, laughing, wrapped in her bathrobe; me by the radio, shedding Armani—shirttails flapping loose, tie around the skull—razing the minibar of every last cocktail and dancing like a fool to "Yakety Yak" . . .

TAKE OUT THE PAPERS AND THE TRASH!

The Coasters. 1958, Spark Records. One minute and fifty seconds of sublime, in-your-face, balls-out nonsense. Everything rock and roll was meant to be . . .

The saxophone solo—the *first* one—sent us bopping around the room in a line. By the second, Greetz had assumed a headstand, jammed in a copper-topped wastebasket/ashtray. His inevitable crash took a phone stand with it. Followed by a half-empty bottle of wine . . . Louise, from above, blasted his manhood—though splayed on the floor in a hot-pink tutu with clusters of cigarette butts in his scalp, it was clear to see that Tinsel's manhood was anything *but* priority one . . .

An urgent pounding let out at the door. Greetz rolled back on a shoulder, flipped up. Stumbled across the room, hollering, "Hold your water! I'm coming, I'm coming!" He opened up and *towered*—wheezing, wild-eyed—over a terrified bellhop. *"DON'T YOU GIVE ME NO DIRTY LOOK!"*

*

Slam.

He wheeled back in / two middle fingers thrown straight to the ceiling . . .

Moments later, the phone started ringing. He stomped to it, picked up, pulled a quick about-face. "*What?*" he balked. "Why, that's ridiculous! Who suggested this? . . . No, no— never mind—I'll get to the bottom of the matter personally!"

He hung up.

"All right." Turning. "They're pissed. Twelve calls in the last five minutes. We've got to figure something out here." He walked to the door and opened it. "COWARDS!" he yelled down the hall.

Slam.

He came back. "What should we do?"

"Any ideas?"

He leapt to the couch. "Isn't there a roof?"

"Screw the roof. Two miles over Siberia? No way!"

"Yes, screw the roof!" said Louise.

Tinsel and I had a good one at that . . .

"All right," he accepted. "Forget the roof. But what does that leave us, then? A lounge?"

"There's a pool and a weight room," I said.

"Screw the weight room!" she came again.

Tinsel broke down, shaking his head. "Such *filthy* talk for a pretty flower!"

She caught him across the face with a two-handed woodcutter's swing of a goose-down pillow. He fell over sideways, clipping a lamp, and dropped to the carpet, under attack.

"Never call me flower!" She bore down repeatedly.

"All right, all right!" he pleaded between blows. "The pool, then! For fuck's sake, the POOL!"

"Besides," she added, "you need another *bath*!"

"Fine, then. OW! Come on—ease up! . . . OW, damn it. *Seriously!* . . . Help me, Chuck!"

"No way," I refused. "That's what you get. In *fact*—" I went for a cushion myself. He curled up, yelling. We pummeled him flat.

Louise's pillow exploded. Feathers all over the floor. "*Espece de con!*" Disgusted, she dropped it and ran out the door. Grabbing a bottle, we followed her lead. Down three flights to the twentieth landing. Out at the lounge, across the rec room. Up to the pool gates: CLOSED FOR THE EVENING.

The lights were out, doors shut tight. A pile of deck chairs stacked in the corner. Street light coming through the windows inside, shimmering over the water's surface.

"This one's open!" Tinsel whispered, testing the door to his left. "Yes." He quietly gestured to *keep it down* . . . Louise ignored him, blowing past . . . Once inside, she dropped her robe and, screaming, carelessly jumped in the pool. I followed along, leaving Tinsel behind—the "cautious one"— shown up as an amateur . . .

Setting the bottle of Scotch on a table, I stripped to the buck, thinking: *Now we're talkin'!* . . .

Tinsel dove into the pool ahead of me. The water went oily brown around him. He sidestroked over to Louise in the deep end . . . I flooded them both with a backward cannon ball. They came up spluttering, lunging about. I got to Greetz and dunked him clean. Louise leapt onto my back and clung tight—every inch of that streamlined body, slick to the touch and pearly-white immaculate, wrapped around and intertwined with my own . . . I stumbled to the shallow end, reeling in bliss. Greetz caught up and plowed us both under. She loosened her grip and slipped away. My back went cold in her absence. Gone.

I crawled from the pool, skulked for the bottle. Tinsel, below, yelling: "Chuck's got love nuts!"

I hovered over him, Scotch in hand, sullenly leering down between hits.

"Cupid digs dark meat, too!" he whinnied.

I capped the bottle, wound up and threw. It clipped his shoulder. He cried out: "OW!" Gripping an arm in pain. "Jesus, *what*?" he sniveled. "Take it easy!"

I glowered: *Cheap, smarmy bastard—lucky she doesn't speak Swahili . . .*

Louise in the background, giggling woozily, climbed from the water and walked down the platform. Turning away so as not to gawk, I wound up facing a wall-length mirror. Her figure, cutting through patches of light, glowed as a crescent moon on the harbor—flashing from cheek to shoulder in swirls, the length of her back in a gentle arc, downward to hip. to thigh. to calf. to ankle. receding . . .

Exquisite mechanics.

Finally, Tinsel cut the whining. "Is that a Pepsi machine?" he asked.

I looked down. "Where?"

He pointed left. I spotted the unlit dispenser. "It's Coke."

"Same shit. Let's throw it in the pool."

I glanced at Louise—over by the diving board, donning her robe.

"Hey, Babette!" called Greetz.

She glared.

"*Whoops.*" He snickered. "You mind if we throw the machine in the water?"

She frowned at Tinsel, then, nodding to me: "Go on—*quickly.*"

Whatever she said . . .

Tinsel climbed out of the water, dripping. We walked to the dispenser, took position. He dropped to one knee, tore a hose from the wall. I followed his lead on my end.

"You ready?" he asked.

"Yeah. Go."

Straining and heaving, we started forward. Chunks of plaster tore from the deck. Bottles rattled inside the machine . . . We kept on pushing, hideous, fugly: scarred by years of debauchery, rot.

Finally, the edge. We tipped the machine. It tore to the pool bed, rocked the whole building. Every patch of the ceiling was sprayed. Tinsel and I were blown out by the tide. The sunken dispenser gurgled at depth, lodged on an incline, upside down . . .

Greetz, whooping, shot out the exit. Louise, behind him: "Hurry up, Charlie!" I got to my feet and followed, slinging Armani, the Scotch, Big Jim and the twins . . .

❊   ❊   ❊

Delayed in the stairwell trying to get dressed. Then forgetting which *floor* we were on . . . By the time I was back in the room, "decent," Tinsel had already staked out the window. I walked to his side for a look of my own. He drew the panel and stepped away.

Down in the street, it was closing on show time. Production appeared to be right on schedule. Scores of technicians ambled about, putting final touches all over the set—some running cables to central generators, others lubing down camera tracks . . . Up at the corner, a pack of Spruce Street lesbians stood, roped off by a guard—awaiting, it seemed, a glimpse of the picture's leading actress . . . What was her name? . . . I couldn't remember—some hot-commodity L.A. starlet everyone knew . . . They were in for a wait, those courageous lesbians, braving the cold in a giddy huddle. Corollo wouldn't show until five minutes shy of the clapboard's drop, the Starlet even later . . .

This never would've happened in the old days.

The material for which Delvin Corollo would be remembered—all his major, or at least *important*, works—had been completed twenty years earlier on a shoestring budget with a limited crew. Meaning: he'd made his mark as an angry young man, and a fairly broke one, at that. Whereas *now:* looking down on the corporate circus of cranes and sandbags and trailers and roadies, you just couldn't help but *know* this production, despite its astronomical budget, would never amount to anything worthy of *Mad Dog La Motta* or *Brutal Roads*. Okay, overstating the obvious, maybe. But the question remained: what's a goatboy to do? Greetz and I could not sit back and allow this crime to proceed unhindered. Not with our present bearings. No way. We were morally bound to sabotage *everything* . . . In fact, we owed it to Delvin himself, as the former artist behind this sham. True, we were doing no better ourselves, but hey . . .

That's what fans are for.

Tinsel, backing away from the window, began to draw up inventory. From twenty-three stories and gravity's boon overhead, the possibilities varied — lamp shades, bottles, mattresses, milk bombs — but nothing quite seemed to cut it, somehow. And meanwhile, the clock was ticking. Out of ideas, I turned away.

Louise, crashed on the sofa behind me — knees pressed together, head tilted back. Grinning in taxed exhilaration. Positively radiant. Grinning at *me*. No one had ever regarded me thus. Try as I did, it was hard to accept. I still couldn't fathom her stake in this matter, much less contend with my own good fortune . . . However, beyond a certain point, the truth was simply stranger than fiction. Right there in front of me. Matching my gaze. Reflecting my rapture. Lovestruck in turn . . . All I could do was stare back, overjoyed, twelve leagues from nowhere with visions of recovery.

She beckoned. I froze, uncertain. She gestured again, patting the couch. I slowly walked over and sat down beside her. She turned to face me, shifting her knees. We stared at each other, not saying a word. A skittish, fluttering ache rolled through me . . . Taking my hand, she pulled me forward and gently nestled my head to her breast. Her skin smelled of apricot, coconut, hope. Her fingers ran over my brow, stroking. Her heartbeat fluttered against my cheek. Life was so damn sweet, it hurt . . .

But Tinsel, of course, interrupted before I could drift any further. Buzzkill Greetz. "*Urrggh!*" He tensed at the window, bouncing up and down on his toes. "Charlie!"

Louise let go of my hand, smiling. I didn't want to leave, but her gaze assured me *Not to worry, all is well—what's meant to be will be, will be* . . .

"Come on!" he insisted. "I think we're in business . . ."

Disinterested now, I walked to the window.

Down below, the crowd had gone silent. Some guards were drawing a rope at the corner. A long black limousine rolled into view. It edged through the gap and stopped beside a crane. The front door opened. A chauffeur appeared. Another guard joined him, scanning the perimeter. Together, they turned and nodded to the limo . . .

A figure in black stepped out to the curb.

"CHEESE DOG!" both of us yelled in synch.

Tinsel grabbed his bullhorn, turning. "Get your camera!" he ordered Louise.

She opened her bag and slid up beside us—"Okay" —producing a handheld recorder.

"We rolling?" He checked.

She leveled the lens. "You're rolling."

"Good. Remember this, now—"

He cranked the horn, leaned out the window and blasted downward: **"COROLLO FUCKS SHEEP!"**

It boomed across the set like a thunderbolt. All heads turned. Every guard looked up. The figure froze in his tracks, cringing. It *was* Corollo. His profile blown . . .

The Spruce Street lesbians bayed like hooligans. Some of the crew technicians laughed. Louise, behind her camera, joined them, as Tinsel and I prepared to unload.

❈ ❈ ❈

Five minutes later, the Starlet arrived to find all of Main in a state of upheaval: set guards scrambling this way and that, some yodeling weirdo at twelve o'clock high and a riotous squad of burly-girthed lesbians mobbing her limo in starstruck bloodlust . . . No more than two hundred people in view, yet all of them seemingly out of their minds . . . Of course, it caught her completely off guard. She drew from the window, shielding her face. Corollo angrily ordered her out. But she wouldn't comply, just sat there, terrified.

Tinsel and I bombarding the crew with senseless abuse from our aerial pulpit—both too soused to throw off a good one, neither faring much better with threats. Settling then on classless jabs (Tinsel: "Blow the honky pork sword!") and smart-ass one-liners (Me: "Nice mustache—you look like a Doobie Brother!") culled from the gutter. Nothing outstandingly clever about it, except for the Cabs— *"Hidey, hidey, hidey HO!"* . . . But it got to Corollo all the same. Before too long, it *overtook* him. In blazing spurts, he threw off a slew of commands, asserting his place at the helm. He pointed a gang of technicians to post, his guards upstairs to silence the monkeys, the Starlet the fuck out of hiding at once . . . All, it appeared, to no effect. Even the hotel's doormen ignored him . . . Seeing as much, he went gung-ho ballistic, storming across the set in a fury. Up to the limo. He opened its door. Dragged the Starlet across the road. Stuffed her into a horse-drawn carriage. The dykes let out with a murderous boo. Tinsel yodeled another Cab Calloway. Delvin waved for the two of us to *can* it. Greetz waved back. Louise kept rolling . . .

We wrecked take one beyond hopes of recovery. Nothing on earth would salvage the mess. And with the dykes lobbing Tastykakes onto the set — I guess they thought they were gobbing, somehow — the visual footage was totaled as well. *Revenge of the Peanut Gallery,* they'd call it . . .

Corollo, already choking with rage, soon caught a milk bomb square in the face. With that, he lost what remained of his cool: blindly flailing from curb to curb — tarred and feathered, Napoleonic homicidal — snaring his coat on a camera pole, falling down flat on his face, recouping, then pointing his guards to go *kick the living shit out of those assholes in the window* . . . Upon which a rent-a-cop broke from his stupor and made for the lobby, unsheathing a stick.

Tinsel closed the window and turned. "All right," he said. "The party's over!" He flew to the closet, grabbed a hanger. Louise lowered the camera. He whirled on her. "NO!"

"But my boots. My purse and bags . . ."

"Don't worry. Charlie'll get 'em. Just stay with the shot!"

"Okay." She resumed.

"And you! Half-breed! Robe it and scoot!"

"Don't yell at me, bastard! *You're* not dressed."

He flashed the coat hanger. "First things first!" Then ran out the door. A smash resounded. "Fucking HELL!"— his voice from the hall. Reappearing, streaked with paint: "*Third* time I've done that!" He shut the door, then hovered in breathless expectation.

A honking staccato blast erupted from every wall. Tinsel went ape—careening around the suite on a gamboling blitz of jabber that ran to the point of: *We're out of the breadline and into the ranks for a NOBEL this time, Charlie,* etc . . .

It was four A.M. Every soul in the building was now obligated to evacuate.

Snapping to, I gathered Louise's luggage, then helped to pull on her boots. The Anarchist grabbed her purse from the table. "One more shot of the street!" he yelled. We looked out the window, tracking a column of sirens blaring down on the set. Cameramen probing the skyline for bombers. The Starlet fleeing the scene under guard. A fight breaking out at the corner of Spruce. Corollo staggering ruefully about . . .

I turned to Louise. She had me on frame. "Say hi, Charlie!"

"Nuke Texas."

Out in the hallway, doors flew open. Horrified voices, volleying, frantic. "*What IS this*?"—Demands.—"*Who's in charge here?*"—"Concern."—*expected to STAND out there?*"—

Panic. — "*ARE we?*" — Outrage. — "*THIS WAS SUPPOSED TO BE FIVE-STAR LODGING!*"

And through it all, the alarms continued — horned to the core of every threshold.

Cracking the door, we peered out just as a walleyed bellhop emerged from the stairwell. Trembling, he launched into fire procedures, only to meet with a tide of disdain. "*Do you have any idea, sir, of WITH WHOM you are speaking?*"

Two rooms down, an elderly woman swooned and cawed of the towering inferno . . . But no one else bought it. Not for a second. There *was* no inferno, no danger at all — just some lunatics in one of these rooms or another — yet still, at 4:05 on the clock, two hundred yards over downtown Anchorage, trapped in the throes of an air-raid drill with every last elevator down for the running, this cheeky fuckwit now had the gall to suggest we dress *warmly:* "This may take time."

*   *   *

Whatever transpired on Main Street during our long, chaotic downward exodus — groping over luggage racks, caught on each landing, madly adrift in the panic tide — Tinsel ahead of us, robed in a bedsheet; Louise behind him, shielding the camera; me to the rear, toting her baggage, doing my best to appear inconvenienced — stumbling onward, clogged and winding, elbow to elbow each step of the way, till the stairwell's ponderous, smothering grind gave way to the full pandemonium of the lobby — chandeliers swinging from the ceiling in the uproar, clerks running by in overwrought fren-

zies, all three front desks tied up and raging, hundreds of
guests come together by the fountain—some of them outright *refusing* to leave, others threatening legal action—wind
blowing in from the street behind them, kicking up night-
shirts, howling, inevitable—with no way to jam a crowd of
four hundred through a single fire door, one by one, every-
body *had* to leave via the lobby, even though the lobby was
blocked by a film set—whatever occurred throughout that
long, cacaphonic interim, none of us knew. Just one thing
was certain: the scene outside came four turns beyond what
anyone expected . . .

With a swarm of fire trucks approaching from the
north, adding to the entourage already present, the hotel's
alarm still screaming unabated and the roar of the crowd at
twenty-five decibels, all of Main seemed a zone under siege.
There must have been eighty-five cops on hand. Up toward
Spruce, they'd convened to deliberate, shouting back and
forth in confusion . . . A tall black crane rose over the
conflict, its long arm crawling with terrified droogs. Down
below, some medics sat tending to a rent-a-cop, plucking
shards of glass from his scalp. Behind them, several dykes
were lined up to the wall, being cuffed and read their
rights—while a thickening group in the middle of it all,
maybe fifteen in total, was *really* going at it: squad chiefs,
firemen, concierges, johnny—kicking up hell and losing
ground fast . . . From what I could gather, it seemed they
were ordering the film crew to pack up and move the set . . .
But Corollo's droogs understandably refused, claiming *no
one* this side of Billings was about to wreck ninety-five hours
of preparation for a blatantly obvious false alarm—especially

not some threadbare posse of beer-gutted schlubs in under-funded wheelbarrows . . .

And all the while, the crowd kept coming, hundreds of outraged, wild-eyed debutantes spilling through the lobby doors into the street . . . And with no one there to lead them away, they stumbled and fell over everything in view, wrecking the set, cursing and yelling—demanding, berating, bewailing, incensed . . .

This had gone *way* too far.

I didn't know *who* clobbered the rent-a-cop. I didn't know *how* the deskmen had gotten involved. I didn't know *what* the dykes were on, or *why* they'd been so gung ho in the first place. I didn't know *when* the police had started deploying all units on routine fire calls. And I didn't know *where* Greetz was going—darting and weaving his way through the crowd . . . Something had obviously gone awry, but at this point, the answer was lost in time. (*Time* for us to be moving along). I only knew that we had to get out . . . In fact, it seemed that Greetz had just done the honors – he *did* love his exits—rounding the corner of Spruce as a fleeting cross of Casper and Pigpen—possibly chasing the Starlet's limo for one last hurrah, as she was gone, too . . .

The party really *was* over.

What had begun as *a(n)-okay-dumb-but-not-altogether-meaningless* prank had taken a pinwheel turn for the ugly, the sour, the violent, the unjustifiable . . . In fifteen minutes, we'd managed to rope in several hundred potential assassins. A Coke machine lodged in the pool up there, on the twentieth floor, had our names all over it—a streak of paint on Louise's door with scores of complaints to back *that,* too. And if *any* of us wound up fingered for *this* . . .

I couldn't let *her* go to prison in Philth Town.

I looked around. She was standing behind me, face downturned, clutching her ribs. Something was wrong, I sensed it immediately. Both of her legs had gone blue in the cold . . .

I tore off my jacket and draped it around her. "Damn it, I'm sorry—you're freezing, Louise."

She shook her head. "That's not it." Quivering, she looked up. "I think something's wrong with me . . ."

"What?" I leaned in.

"I think . . ." She stared at her forearms, confused. I followed her gaze. She scratched one wrist, drew back and frowned, then scratched some more. "*I think I've got bugs!*"

"*What?*" I almost broke down laughing. The thought of Louise with bugs was absurd. "What the hell are you talking about?"

"I'm serious!" She straightened up. "Where is he?"

"Who?"

"That friend of yours, dirty—" Twitching, she broke off. "My God, it's *horrible!*"

"Hold on a second."

"And where's my *camera?*" she demanded. "My purse!"

I looked at her bags. "But I thought . . ."

"WHAT?"

". . . *you* had the camera."

"No! *He* took it!"

"On our way out the door?"

"In the stairs!" she shouted.

"Okay."

"Where *is* he?"

"I'll find him."

"Don't *touch* me!"

"Sorry! I'm sorry . . ."

Scanning the crowd, she kneaded and clawed her torso, sick with the heebie-jeebies. Essence of Greetz, having marred the backdrop, had now infiltrated her inner sanctum . . .

"I'll find him," I tried to assure her. "Don't worry."

She ripped off the jacket and handed it back. "I knew I shouldn't have given him this!"

"What? My coat?"

"No, this robe!" Twitching in horror. "He wore it last night, the sick degenerate . . ." She broke off again. Then: "Don't you feel it? He was in *your* room."

"*My* room?" I said. "But I thought you two—"

"—took it while I fashioned your bandage," she continued, "pacing the floor, drinking and yelling, pawing like an animal . . . I finally had to lock him in with *you* to get some sleep. And look at me *now*! I've got bugs, Charlie!" She kicked the curb. "I've got fucking *bugs*!"

I stepped back, letting her rave for a moment. Slowly, everything drifted together: her robe, her camera, the purse, her tickets, passport, keys and wallet, the cooties . . . Tinsel, asleep in the bed to my left. Under *lock and key* . . . His:

"Wouldn't you?" My: "friend says a lot of things—" Her, with a grin: "I'm sure he does . . ."

Lied to me. Turncoat. Bald-faced. Point-blank. Shifty-eyed. Treacherous Rotten Bastard . . .

When all this time I'd known, instinctively, far beyond the pale of doubt: there was no way in *hell* Louise would *ever* bed down with the Anarchist. *Zero chance* . . . The notion alone was a crime against virtue; the fact that I'd even *considered* it, shameful. Louise would have slapped me across the face had she—

Jarred from my rage by the sound of her voice: "Come on, let's GO!" She grabbed my wrist. "I can't. take. one. more. *minute* of this!"

"Go?"

"To a shower!"

"Your car—"

"FORGET the car! PLEASE, Charlie! HELP me here!" She tightened her grip. "Take me to your place."

"The Desmon?"

"What*ever*!"

"But my room . . ."

"Your room?"

"It's a mess."

"I don't *CARE*!"

I picked up her bags. She dragged me along. A skirmish broke out to one side. We dodged it. Coming around, she tripped on a suitcase. Scandinavian tourists, bawling. She fired back in their native tongue. I pried them apart, taking the lead. We got to the corner. A taxi appeared, by the ides of Crom. We hailed it. Off duty . . . Louise in the road. The driver stopped. Flashing my wallet, I opened a door. She got in. I turned for one final look . . .

Things would be different on coastal New Guinea.

FINALE

Dojo was wide awake at seven. The Feeders had kept him up all night. He answered the door on a rocket-fuel high, his gleaming skull roped off by a draw chain. "*Who?*" he challenged.

"Charlie," I said.

His mangled lips hung unresponsive. "Charlie," he muttered. Then: "Evans!" It caught. "Hanoi Jackson!" rang through the stairwell. He rattled the chain. The door flew open. "Hell, I thought the party was over!"

I stepped inside. The air stank of gas.

"Pardon the fumes," he explained. "Napalm."

"*Napalm?*"

"Sure." He held out a rag.

I winced.

He laughed. "Figured not. A smart one, you—never *have* gone for deep fry." Turning away, he bolted the door. "The rest of these fools can't seem to get enough. Just look what they did to my kitchen, bastards . . ."

*

True, his flat had been thrown for a whirl—sofas up-
ended, garbage everywhere. Globs of mayo smeared on the
wall. Cigarette burns on a print of Il Duce . . .

Dojo swept some cans from the table, grabbed a chair
and dropped it in place. "Have a seat. What can I get you?"

"A piece."

"What?" He paused. "For the *sewers*?"

"No," I said. "We're done with that."

"Oh." He scratched his head. "No questions . . ."

"Yeah, if it's all the same."

"It is." He shrugged. "For *you* it is . . . My dad always
told me, whatever happens, 'The less you know, the less they
can find out.'" He walked to the closet, pulling out a key.
"Of course, the old man died in *jail* . . ." he added. "But that's
neither here nor there. The essential thing is trust. Right?
With some of these people, it's not so easy." He shook his
head, unlocking the door. "Just the other night, a guy came
by. One quick look and I knew he was trouble. You can always spot a cuckold. And cuckolds are snitches . . . So I asked
what he planned on doing with the heat, and he tells me 'kill
my wife'—straight out—'put a bullet through her head.' You
believe this guy? I mean, what do I look like—a fucking
shmoo?"

"So what happened?" I asked.

He pointed to a bottle. "Chloroform. Left him for
Smokey outside."

"*You* called the cops?"

"Yeah. Don't spread it . . ."

He lifted a box from the highest shelf. "Okay, let's see." He set it on the table. His fingers flexed. "Something special?"

"No, just small."

"Small," he mumbled, picking and sifting. "How's a twenty-two sound?"

"Not *that* small."

"Okay. Maybe this?" He produced a .380. "Only fired once."

"Yeah?" I looked at it. "What about the brown one?"

"The Glock?" He frowned. "Nah. Glitchy. Besides, it's not mine."

"All right." I kept digging. "Then how's the nine?"

"The what?" He turned. "Oh God, *that*! NO! Do yourself a favor, Charlie—stay away from that one."

"Why? Too pricey?"

"*Hell* no. I ought to *pay* someone to take it off me."

"Why?" I asked. "What's the story?"

"You don't want to know . . ."

"Really? *That* bad?"

"Trust me. Forget it."

"How much?"

"Eighty."

I gave him a hundred. "And add a mask."

"A mask?"

"Nixon."

"*Nixon?*"

"Richard."

He scratched his head. "I've only got Thatcher."

❊

And Thatcher it was, though torn and moldy — one ear missing, a hole in the forehead . . . I tried her on. "This thing is filthy," I yelled from inside.

"Yancey wore it giving head last night."

I tore at the rubber.

He laughed. "Just kidding. Want a bump for the road? You look like you need one."

I toweled the nine, tucked it. "All right."

He grabbed a mirror, dumped some powder. "Oh!" He grinned while chopping lines. "I meant to ask, we've *all* been wondering —" A bead of sweat rolled down his nose. "*Who* was that fox with you guys at Maxine's?"

"My lawyer," I said.

"*Yeah*. Your lawyer."

"It's true."

"Uh-huh. And I'm the pope." He rolled up a dollar, passed it. "Careful . . ."

We blasted, shook hands.

"So long, Evans."

❊   ❊   ❊

Back in my room. Louise out cold. The shower had done her a world of good. With a dirty old sheet pulled over one shoulder, she looked to be sleeping off multiple air strikes.

Drawing the blinds, I sat for a minute. Ned on the wall. Staring impatiently. One of these days I'd fly to Glenrowan and drink a bottle of Scotch at the inn.

❊

I got up and gathered some clothes from the corner —
pants, a jacket, an old pair of boots. Stuffing them into a
burlap sack, I walked out the door and locked it behind me.

❊   ❊   ❊

Nothing happening down in the lobby. Seven-twenty-five
on the clock. Phone off the hook, no sign of Jones. Unbolt-
ing the exit, I stepped outside.

The crank hit home at the top of the staircase: hot
sweats, palpitations, lockjaw, the shakes. I'd only done meth
on three occasions — this time around to clear my head. Fifteen hours of nonstop boozing had taken its toll. The edge
was gone. A boost for the coming ordeal had seemed fitting.
But *damn* if I hadn't forgotten the *rush* . . .

I stood in the half-light, gnawing my tonsils. The morning air felt plastic, foul. My fingers jittered. I spat in the
gutter. The Row was quiet. *Except* for the Swillery . . .

All right, here went —
Three steps.

One.

I crossed the scrap lot, heap by heap, sticking with the
shadows to the edge of Dowler. From there I held a good
lock on the store — a wraparound view of the whole facade . . . Hanz up front, counting the till, his profile etched
in lavender neon. The main door chained, gates drawn tight,
the sidewalk-side cellar hatch locked and barred . . . Everything closed on the entrance side. But the back was open.

Right on schedule. Hanz's Chrysler parked by the curb, its trunk stacked with Michelob, keys in the slot. A brand-new clerk — my replacement, Chinese — shoveling stock through the open door.

From behind the hulk of a rotting fridge, I waited for the elevator's automated bell. Once it rang, I crossed the avenue. Got to the Chrysler. Grabbed its keys. Slammed the trunk, first checking the road. Then shot through the stock door, closed it tight . . .

The elevator was on B, down in the cellar. I called. It responded. The door slid open. No sign of the clerk . . . Tough break, that one — his first day and all. But necessity dictates . . .

Blocking the door with a stack of soda, I was sure to *jam* the elevator this time. Then I wheeled out the errand bike and removed a graphite lock from its frame. Moving along, I pulled the nine. Donned Thatcher. Slipped on gloves. Opened the door. Crept down the hallway. Onto the main floor, hugging a rack . . .

The Dutchman must have heard me coming. His till slid shut. "Em-ah, Li! Howz't going?"

I stood by the beer case, holding my breath.

"Li!" he repeated, more flustered than worried.

I stepped into view. He threw up his hands. I pointed the nine. He dove from the plank. I grabbed his collar. He squealed like a pig. I kicked him in the gut. "*Shut your mouth!*" Then dragged him along. He wiggled and thrashed. I pulled out the U-lock.

"Please!" he squawked.

"SHUT THE FUCK UP!"

He pissed himself—all over the floor.

I backed off, scowling. "Keep it together!"

Skirting his flow, I unfastened the lock and clamped his neck to a lower rack. He lay there, bound and contorted, helpless, both eyes bulging through cracked bifocals. In two or three hours, they'd free him with a saw—its circular blade just grazing his throat. By then I'd be halfway over the schlock belt, picking through my in-flight turkey pot pie.

I drew the blinds, cut the phone. Emptied the register. Bagged its cash. Returned to the stockroom. Killed the lights. Shut the back and got in the Chrysler.

Not bad at all. Three minutes, total. No complications. Now for the Anarchist.

Two.

It was dawn when I got to the river. The opposite freeway hummed with activity. A wash of gray spread over the skyline, speckled with jet streams, smokestacks and gulls.

I parked the car at the edge of the yard. Dropped the cash in the trunk and locked it. Threw the sack over my shoulder, then crossed the tracks and made for the bridge.

As always, Tinsel was hiding dockside, stationed beneath the overpass. Anytime one of his schemes went awry, it was off to the river once again. He'd slept down here more

than any tramp. Half of the trash in the yard was his. The
torn wool blanket thrown over his legs had been stolen from
Zelda's apartment last winter.

"Took you long enough." He spoke without looking,
holding his gaze on the river. "Of course, then again—" He
shook his head. "I was starting to wonder if *you'd* show at all."

Louise's purse lay open beside him, its contents scattered
and smashed on the platform. The wall above him was
streaked with lipstick: thick red swirls reading: *Ha Ha Ha . . .*

He pulled out the camera, opened its screen. A flicker-
ing glow spread over his face. "You've gotta see this." He
pressed a button. "I told her we'd make a good film in the
States."

A gull flew by. I watched it go. Another one dropped
from the bridge, tossing. Together, they cleared the opposite bank, then floated north, bound for the station.

"Ah!" He sat up. "Here we are. Yeah, that's perfect.
Look at her, Chuck." He angled the screen my way, then
wiggled a finger at the image. "Stupid skirt. Yes, you're
beautiful. Yes, look at you. And such a figure . . ." The
cooing ended. "A shame you can't work it. Put a man to
sleep . . ."

"Tinsel—"

"Hold on!" He raised one hand. "I wanna see this part
again . . . Yeah—right here. When I take the camera . . . Ha!
Christ! What a *sucker.*"

Enough.

I dropped the sack at his feet.

He looked up. "What's this?"

"Clothes. Get dressed."

"Why?"

"We've got twenty minutes."

"Twenty minutes till *what*?"

"Till the Farmer's First on Elm Street opens."

Leering, he cocked his head and spat. "Don't patron-
ize me."

"I'm not," I assured him. "You wanted a car—" I
jangled the keys. "You needed a pistol—" I held out the nine.
"You asked for a mask—" I pulled up Thatcher. "And someone should drive. *I'll* see to that."

He looked me over, awaiting the catch. When nothing
hit, the leer receded. Soon he was sniffing the bait in earnest, beaming suspicion: *too good to be true.*

"You jerkin' my cord?" he finally demanded.

"Not at all. I'm game. Let's do it."

He slapped the platform, jumped to his feet. "Well all
right, then!" Dropping the blanket. "At last—someone with
real cojones!" He picked up the sack. "I *knew* you'd come
through."

I turned away, looked down on the river. A fish was
encased in the ice below. Part of its back and a fin protruded,
nicked and torn by hungry gulls.

"You know," he remarked, "I've got to admit—you had
me worried for a while there, Breed. From where I was
standing, it seemed Babette had the hooks in you good. I
mean, don't get me wrong—I knew you'd come to your
senses in time. Sooner or later, reason would hit . . . But the
moment I spotted you two on the couch, I really had to

wonder: *has Chuck lost his mind?*" He plowed through the sack, grabbing a shirt. "'Course, then I realized what was happening."

"Oh?" I asked. "And what was that?"

"Simple," he answered. "You were just workin' it. Why not, anyhow? More power to you! Nobody wants out of Dodge like Charlie. So peddle your ass for a day in exchange. The kingdom was founded by drunkards and whores. All you had do was play lapdog for Madame, who *did* love the way you stroked that fiddle . . . And next thing going, you're off to New Guinea! No harm done, right? Everything works out: you get passage, I get a piece, she gets the shaft and we all fall down . . ." Grinning, he flashed some plastic. "The only question is: what happens to the gold card?"

I pulled out a cigarette.

"Gimme one of those?"

I tossed him the pack.

"Thanks." He fired up. "I just wish I'd been there to see the rest. The look on her face . . . *What? . . . Who, me? . . . How could this* happen?" He threw back, laughing. "Stupid skirt."

"Can I see that card?"

"Sure. Hold on to it. There's also a passport somewhere in there. I know a guy in Jersey who can doctor it up.'"

"I thought that was no longer possible," I said.

"*Bah!*" He pulled on the jacket. "Anything's possible. Send you to Chile as 'Louis Gascoygne.' All too easy. Would I lie to you?"

Patience . . .

"Here." He threw me the purse. "There's an AmEx, too. Probably still active. And *what*, pray tell?" He held up the mask. "I asked for Dick."

"Pardon that."

He shrugged. "Doesn't matter. Nixon, Thatcher—"

Here it came . . .

"Same shit, right?"

Three.

We drove down Elm in the Chrysler. Traffic was sparse, most everything closed. My shakes had gradually stiffened to palsy: every joint in the system locked. The sweats were gone, along with my chills. But the nausea lingered, no thanks to Greetz.

"Lookit that scrub!" he yelled as we passed a tramp in several coats and a helmet. "Somebody ought to hose these dogs!" He came back around, demanding tunes. I switched on the radio. "'Fly by Night'? Screw that, Chuck!" He rolled the dial. It landed on ABBA. *"That's* more like it—Euro, not *white*, trash. Neutral boogie!"

We rounded the corner at Nineteenth Street. Circled the block and parked by a bakery. The Farmer's First was three doors behind us, walk lights on, activity inside.

I flipped the hazards. "You know what you're doing?"

"Yeah," he mumbled. "Time check?"

"Fifty-five."

"Okay." Switching gears. "Here's the deal. They unlock at eight . . . I head in then . . . nix the cameras . . . line up the crowd . . . The tellers'll be counting last night's deposits, so right away, that's in the bag . . . " He cleared his throat, trying to stay with it. "Then," he continued. "*Then . . .*"

"Yeah?"

"*Then*—I'm on it, give me a second—THEN—" He coughed. "You fucked me up—THEN: herd everyone into a corner . . . get a manager on the safe, a teller on the registers and . . . finally, together into the vault. Ten minutes, tops."

"*That's* your plan?" I asked.

"Yeah, why? Got a problem with it?"

"No," I admitted. "Just sounds familiar."

He punched the dash. "I *knew* you'd say that!" Shaking his head. "But listen, Charlie: Sonny was an idiot. This'll be different. Believe me—I'm on it . . ."

"All right." *All the better.* "So what about me?"

"*You* sit tight. Keep your eyes open. And roll the camera . . . If anything happens, honk twice, but don't take off unless you absolutely have to. And when this is over, don't floor it, either. Drive smooth and steady to Twenty-second, hook a right, *then* accelerate. Once on the Parkway, continue to Riverside. Pull off at Deermount, back in that nook . . . We ditch the car, hike through the fields—up to the bridge in no-man's-land. From there we hop the Regional to Kratztown. Some people I know live a block from the station."

He grabbed my wrist to check the time. Exhaled. "I need another smoke."

I handed one over. "Make it quick."

"I know." He shivered. "I love that we're doing this."

❋

ABBA fizzled to muffler commercials. Then came a forecast: snowing in Georgia. I peered out the window, trying to recall a single worthwhile moment with Tinsel . . .

"Don't worry." He nodded. His forehead glared, plastered with locks of grease and hair. "I've got this rehearsed. By Wednesday morning we'll be in Acapulco. You ever been to Mexico?"

I thought of us breaking into the zoo.

"No." He smiled. "You're in for a ride—the women down there *love* rich Americans. Even *your* kind, if you know what I mean—though it might run you extra. Nothing *too* steep." He sucked on the Merit, wincing and jittering. "'Course, if it *is*, you can always just *buy* one—wetback women are cheap and obedient."

Tossing bread to the bears in the moonlight . . .

"Man!" He shifted, straightening out. "I really. Can't. *Believe.* This is happening." Dragging the cigarette, crazed with impatience: "Who you got between an otter and a fox."

And tripped an alarm outside of the birdhouse . . .

"Neither?" he said. "All right, something else. What about a sloth and a koala bear?"

*

Then ran like hell, fleeing a spotlight . . .

"Let me guess," he assumed. "The koala."

"*Please* shut up."

He frowned. "What's wrong?"

"This game is asinine."

"Well," he huffed. "Too bad, Jack. You've got better?"

"*Silence,* maybe."

"That won't do!" He waved me off. "Come on, let's have it!"

Something occurred to me. "All right," I offered. "Greetz and Evans."

He jerked in his seat. "Whooaa! Yeah! Now, *there's* an idea. Good one, Breed." Forgetting the bank for a moment, he declared: "Don't even *dream* about that, understand?" He'd obviously given the question some thought. "You wouldn't survive a round with me."

I held up my hands.

"I'm serious!" he said.

"Yup." I nodded. "Just wanted to hear it."

The radio droned into "I'm a Loser." Tinsel, squirming, changed the subject. "What about resolutions?" he asked.

"What *about* resolutions, Greetz?"

"New Year's resolutions," he said, hacking the words. "Did you make any?"

"No."

"NO?" Attempting to schmooze it out. "A person should always make at least *one . . .*"

I gripped the wheel.

"Want to hear mine?"

He knew I didn't.

"All right, all right . . . Truth is, neither did I. Make one. But I'll tell you what, we're in this together: think of something while I'm inside, and later on we'll see it through. Mutual, like. You know—teamwork! Fortification of mind and body . . . That is, of course, unless you settle on something dumb, like dropping tobacco."

Down the street, a rat shot by. A startled postman leapt out of the way.

Greetz: "You see that carrier"—pointing—"betcha we're gone before he gets to the park."

"Fine," I said.

"How much?"

"Fifty."

"Deal. Let's see it."

"I'm out."

He scoffed. "Typical jive, damn it, Charlie—you're *always* busted. Time and again!" He rolled down the window, blew smoke through the crack. "Even Babette couldn't take any more."

I looked up. "What?"

"That's what she said."

"*What* did she say?"

He paused to reflect. "Last night, it was." His expression narrowed. "Ah! Yes." Squaring away: "She said you were bright, sweet and considerate, but with all due respects, she was sick of footing bills."

I busted out laughing. "Yeah!"

"That's right. *Then* she claimed that it ran in the genes."

"Okay, Tinsel." I shook my head. "Whatever you say . . ."

Jesus Christ.

By now it seemed the look on my face would've blown the plan. But apparently not. Despite my ill-concealed disgust, Greetz remained in a world of his own. I guess the evening had gone to his head. Selling his shtick no longer mattered. *That* was the part that really got me: I didn't appear to warrant the effort.

"Listen—" Something tore in his throat. "I don't bring this up to get your dander."

"Well, why *do* you bring it up? Tell me. *Please.*"

"I'm just trying to say things'll change now, see. We clear seven figures and the bitches go color-blind."

Something clanged in the street behind us. We turned.

A clerk was unlocking the door.

"Okay," said Tinsel, grabbing the pistol. "Is this thing loaded?"

"And *cocked.* You're set."

"All right." He flicked his smoke out the window, then rubbernecked, probing. "You see anyone?"

"No. It's clear."

He pulled on the mask. "Then this is it . . ." He opened the door, stepped out and turned. "All Hail Discordia!"

"Just get going."

He crept to the bakery wall and followed it clear to the bank, then darted inside.

＊

Originally, I'd planned to sit for a minute—at least till the blinds dropped, just for good measure. But once he was gone, that changed. Timing be damned—I could wait no longer. The Chrysler's interior stunk so badly of all things Tinsel, I *had* to get out.

I grabbed Louise's purse and camera. Crossed the street. Found a phone, sank a quarter. 911: "How may I direct you?"

"Police," I garbled, cupping the receiver.

Beethoven's Ninth. Static interference . . .

I looked at the bank. The charges tolled:

- Grand larceny (the Farmer's First)
- Kidnapping (confinement of bank staff)
- Malicious mischief (tampering with cameras)
- Receipt of stolen goods (the nine)
- Grand theft auto (the Swillery mobile)
- Petty larceny ($152 from register, in trunk)
- Simple assault (battery of Dutchman)
- Aggravated assault (*with* a deadly weapon)

"This is Sergeant Eugene Clark . . ."

- The judge's imperative: "fifty to life"

"This is Sergeant CLARK!" Now with impatience.

I hung up.

＊

I couldn't do it . . .

I had to give him a *chance*, at least: a shot at the 5 percent—more than he rightly deserved, perhaps. So was
prison.

Therefore, only advantage(s):

1) Keys in ignition, a full tank of gas—can't say I left
him *entirely* screwed. With any luck, he *might* get away. If
not, he could always plead insanity . . .
2) An empty clip, no risk of bloodshed—possible re-
duction of charges thereby. Can't smoke a teller with no ammunition. If nothing else, I still had manners.

And as for *resolutions*—now that we'd broached the subject—a few came to mind. Starting, here, with a hasty retreat, then moving on to the imminent picture . . .

First: return to the Desmon, head off the hammers.
Quickly: avoiding police. Gather cash. Wake Louise. Call a
taxi. Race to the airport. Check her bags. Purchase ticket.
What will be, will be, will be . . .

Cutting it close, no doubt. But hey—I'd already nixed
all basic farewells. Not that any were called for, mind you:
twenty-three years in this god-awful town and nary a part-
ing exchange in order . . .

How?

✽

And (what-else-but) *furthermore:* drop the tobacco . . .

Things would be different <u>now</u>.

✽   ✽   ✽

I reached the park ahead of the carrier. Cleared the southern gate unnoticed. Two blocks on, a cruiser passed. I watched it go.

So long, Greetz.